CHARLEY'S HORSE

JUDITH SHAW

Praise from Readers

I enjoyed this story immensely, especially its scrappy little heroine. Charley is fun and self-deprecating with a dry, irreverent wit. She is quite insightful for an 11-year-old. Because we are privy to her thinking, her comments to herself and the wonderful, unrequited letters she sends to her best friend, one gets to know this smart, honest young girl and her redemptive love affair with her adopted summer horse. A bonus to this engaging story was learning about horses, riding and driving. Not all of this was unfamiliar to me, however, I learned a great deal.
—**Joanne Conroy, Stockbridge, Massachusetts**

This book really brought me back to my time spent at Girl Scout camp. Like Charley, we were sent to get out of our parents' sight. I was also glad the author was completely honest about the nature of horses. I remember my daughter Tamara thinking all horses were like Black Beauty, until she went to take off a bitchy mare's blanket and was bitten on the arm for her trouble.
—**Mary Garabedian, Bradenton, Florida**

The book, set in 1959, puts me at nearly the same age as Charley so I liked the references to that era. I enjoyed reminiscing through Charley's eyes about my childhood love of horses and the anxieties of growing up.
—**Sue Edwards, Windsor, Massachusetts**

Two things: one was the honest emotion of a young girl who has been betrayed on several levels and her determination to work out the solution. The other was the fascinating description of the relationship between horse and rider and the actual mechanics of driving and riding. This overview of the technicalities gave the book an authenticity that someone less knowledgeable and generous could not have provided.

—Diana Ladden, Copake Falls, New York

The story was very compelling and I didn't want to put it down. The characters were believable and interesting, and I thought the tensions between the characters were well balanced and well done. Very interesting plot twists and nuances. I learned a lot about horses and the difficulties of learning to ride. The camp scenes were spot on.

—Donna Lefkowitz, Lenox, Massachusetts

I couldn't put it down. I was captivated right through. I'm a 67-year-old bloke who knows nothing about horses, and I loved it. I found it to be a beautiful story of growth, overcoming fears, dealing with situations and people, and it was all so wonderfully crafted. Always that little hook so that the reader wants to read on and see how it develops.

—Greg McKay, Wentworth Falls, NSW, Australia

I'm still thinking about Charley, and expect I will continue to do so for a long time to come.

—Stewart Edelstein, Stockbridge, Massachusetts

Laughing Dog Press
P.O. Box 203
Great Barrington MA 01230

Author's website: storiesbyjudith.com
To contact the author: storiesbyjudith@gmail.com

For anyone who's ever been in love with a horse.

Acknowledgments

Heartfelt thanks to all the people, old and young, horse lovers and not, who read this manuscript in its many phases. Your comments inspired me to get the lead out and finish the darned thing.

My writing coach, Milli Thornton, shepherded me through all phases of writing and producing *Charley's Horse*. Without her, I wouldn't be writing these acknowledgments.

Last but never least, my family, who hung in there through 25 years of horse obsession and three years of writing this book. My husband Ron fixed miles of fences, put stall doors back on their hinges when the horses broke out, and picked up mountains of horse poop. Without him I would be nowhere.

"A horse, a horse! My kingdom for a horse!"
William Shakespeare
Richard III, Act III, Scene IV

Sheffield, Massachusetts, 1959

I ran to my room and slammed the door, so angry I couldn't see. I lost my balance and crashed into the wall.

My china horses rattled and whinnied at me to settle down.

"*Grateful*?" I sobbed. "I'll show you grateful!"

I swept my arm along the shelf. The screams of injured horses filled the room, blood streaming, legs snapping, hearts breaking. My own legs gave out and I slid to the floor, blinded by my tears.

Chapter One

THE DAY STARTED WITH THE usual stuff. School was just school. Sally's mom picked her up—riding lesson—and gave me a lift home, saving me about an hour of waiting for the bus, sitting on the bus, and walking home from the bus stop. She picked Sally up a lot, so the ride was nothing special, but it was nice to have a little extra time before supper.

We sat in the back seat, noses buried in our books. Sally's mother twirled the dial on the radio, looking for the three o'clock news. When "Misty" came on I interrupted.

"Please, Mrs. Bartlett, can we listen to that? It goes with my book."

"What are you reading, Charlene?"

I made a face. I hate being called Charlene.

"*Misty of Chincoteague.*"

"For about the three hundredth time," Sally said.

"I get misty, just holding your hand," Johnny Mathis sang, in his sweet husky voice. No one spoke until the song was over. "Hound Dog" came on and Mrs. Bartlett changed the station.

"Why do you read that old book over and over?" Sally asked. "Don't you get tired of it?"

Sally gets bored easily. She's a full-speed-ahead, take-no-prisoners sort of person, while I like to hang on to the old and familiar. We've been best friends since kindergarten, but sometimes I have to dig in my heels and stand up for myself.

"I like it," I said, looking back at the page. "I like it that people once lived with horses every day, that kids helped to train them, and rode them to school, and taught them their manners. And I love the part where Paul is in the truck with The Phantom and Misty the night before Pony Penning and falls asleep with Misty in his arms."

Sally had already moved on.

"Can Charley watch my lesson?" She was bouncing in her seat. Sally's never much good at sitting still, and as soon as horses come into the conversation she's a helium balloon tugging at its string. "Please? Pretty please with sugar on it?"

Mrs. Bartlett and I answered at the same time.

"I can't."

"Not today, sweetie."

The last thing I wanted to do was watch her ride. I'd never even met a horse face to face, and I didn't have the strength to watch Sally get my heart's desire.

I waved as the car pulled away. Sally stuck her head out the window. "Maybe next week!" she yelled.

I sincerely hoped not.

We live on a dead-end street in the middle of nowhere. No one in my family is going to drive me to a stable ten miles away, and anyway, I had no money. You can't babysit if there aren't any kids nearby.

I dropped my jacket on the mudroom bench, went to my room and closed the door, waving to the porcelain herd as I walked past. I put *Misty* in her slot on the shelf where all my Marguerite Henry books lived.

It wasn't the only bookcase in the room, but it was the neatest. Three others overflowed with old favorites, new loves, and many, many library books. More than a few were overdue. I like checking books out, but I hate returning them. In third grade I had more overdue library books than anyone in the high school. Maybe a world's record! Not that I'm proud of it or anything.

Sally'd given me the *British Horse Society Complete Horse and Pony Care* for my birthday, and I practically had it memorized. Without a horse to practice on it didn't make a lot of sense, but it would surely come in handy someday.

My favorite book was *Justin Morgan Had a Horse*. I knew in my bones that one day I'd have a Morgan like Feller. I wouldn't care if people thought he was small and undistinguished. I would love him for his huge heart.

I unpacked my schoolbag and organized the day's homework into piles. I'm not really interested in homework, but I like to know what the assignments are.

After a while I got hungry and went to the kitchen. Mom was at the counter wrestling with a chicken. Why wasn't she in the shop? And where was my dad? He's the cook, not Mom.

"Hi, Mom. Need any help?"

"Home already?"

"Mrs. Bartlett gave me a ride with Sally."

"I'm just about done here. You can make the salad later. I'll preheat the oven before I leave, and you can put the pan in at five-thirty. Grab some vegetables from the freezer, and you and Jeremy should be set. Just leave the leftovers. I'll eat when I get back."

"Where are you going? Is Dad home?"

"I should be back around seven. Don't forget to rinse the dishes."

Just that quickly, she was gone. I took a box of

Sugar Smacks out of the pantry, but my appetite had disappeared.

Jeremy came home and went straight to the garage. The chain on his bike had snapped, and he wanted to fix it before the weekend. I needed to talk to him about how strange our parents were getting, but he always acted as if everything was all right. I set the table for four anyway and went back to my room.

We ate supper in front of the TV. I wrapped the untouched chicken in foil and gave my homework a quick once-over. Then I put on pajamas and lay on my bed.

Things were falling apart. I could smell it, but I couldn't *see* it.

I had a ton of questions and no one to ask:

1. Where was Dad?
2. Why was Mom stomping around the house with a stone face and no conversation?
3. What was happening to my family?

The house creaked sleepily but had no answers.

At about ten o'clock I heard the garage door open and shut. Feet tiptoed down the hall and disappeared. Water ran in the shower and stopped. The toilet flushed and hands were washed. Then silence.

It was the middle of the night before I finally fell asleep.

"BREAKFAST! USE IT OR LOSE it!"

For a second I thought everything was back to normal, but the strain in Mom's voice was hard to miss. She sounded hoarse, like she'd been crying.

I got dressed and shoved my books in the schoolbag but passed on breakfast. I could just see myself barfing on the bus. Mom started to say something, but I walked out the door, chewing on the inside of my cheek to keep from crying. A few tears leaked out anyway.

They weren't tears of sadness. They were tears of rage.

Jeremy ran up just as the bus pulled in. He shoved past me and bolted up the steps. He's older, so he thinks he should get on first.

The day was a blur. Teachers came and went. If called on, I answered, sort of, but Mrs. Barkley got the message early that I wasn't really in the classroom. For once, she didn't push it. Even Sally kept out of my way.

The bus ride home lasted forever. I stared out the window but didn't see a thing.

Chapter Two

MOM'S CAR WAS GONE, AND so was Dad's. Jeremy was wherever Jeremy goes. The empty house made me want to cry.

I had Cheerios for supper in my room. I don't know if or what Jeremy ate. He was so busy pretending everything was normal, he probably grilled himself a steak and ate it at the table.

Mom and Dad didn't get home till late. I watched TV, bit my nails, and waited.

I think they were surprised to see me. Maybe they'd planned to sneak in and not confront us until morning.

Mom gave me a disapproving look. "It's a school night. Shouldn't you be in bed?"

I stared her down and stayed where I was.

Dad sighed and sat down on one end of the couch. Mom took the other corner, holding a throw pillow against her stomach like a barricade. The silence stretched, and stretched, and stretched. Then, like a rubber band pulled too far, it snapped.

They both began talking at once, stopped, and looked at each other.

"You have to understand. . . ." Dad started.

Mom interrupted. "Where's Jeremy?"

I shrugged. The last I saw he was headed for the garage and his greasy old bicycle chain. If they wanted him they could go look.

Right on cue, he walked through the back door.

"Come and sit down, son," my father said.

"Over here," Mom said, patting the couch next to her.

Jeremy hung his jeans jacket on its hook and headed for his room.

"Jeremy!" Mom snapped. "Turn around and sit down, please. We want to talk to you both."

For a minute, no one said a word. Then Dad cleared his throat.

"'The time has come,' the Walrus said,
'To talk of many things:
Of shoes—and ships—and sealing-wax—
Of cabbages—and kings—
And why the sea is boiling hot—
And whether pigs have wings.'"

His voice trailed off, but my mind kept going.

O Oysters, come and walk with us!
The Walrus did beseech. . . .

I didn't know what was coming, but it wouldn't be good. Look what happened to the poor oysters.

I chewed on my thumbnail, saw Mom staring at my hand, and stuffed it under my butt.

"Your father and I have decided to live apart," Mom started. "Dad is looking for an apartment and will be moving at the end of the month. You two will stay here, of course. My mother will come to take over the cooking and look after you while I'm at work."

I could feel my jaw drop.

Dad moving out? Gram moving in?

I'd known something was coming, but not this.

"What do you mean, live apart? You're married! You have to live together!"

"We're calling it a trial separation," Mom said, "but don't let the words fool you. We're planning to get a divorce."

I felt like I'd been punched. Only movie stars got divorced. What were they talking about?

Jeremy turned back towards his room.

"Hang on, Jeremy. We're not done here yet."

Jeremy froze but didn't turn around.

My father continued. "This summer is going to be difficult. Your mother and I have a lot of details to work out. It would be better for all of us—especially you two—if we don't have an audience."

Jeremy turned around to stare at them. I studied a small rip in my sneaker.

Mom cleared her throat. "I—that is, *we*—think it would be better for all concerned if you spent the summer at a sleep-away camp. I've done some research and found two camps, one for boys and one for girls, on Beaver Lake outside Weston, Connecticut.

"The camps are run by the same family and share some activities. You'll be able to see each other from time to time. They come highly recommended and should suit you both very well."

Mom sounded like a brochure for Camp Perfect: the place to stash your kids when you don't want them home for the summer. I could feel my face getting hot and had to bite my tongue.

"I know this decision seems sudden, but your father and I have made up our minds. Camp starts in three weeks, and we need to get you two ready to leave."

Dad looked away, but I could see a muscle jumping in his jaw. I stared at him so hard he had to hear my thoughts, but he said nothing.

"I'm not going to camp and you can't make me!"

How did that pop out? I swallowed and tried again.

"Gram doesn't need to move in here," I said as reasonably as I could. "I'm eleven. I can do the cooking and the vacuuming and stuff. I can even clean the bathrooms. Jeremy can go to camp if he wants, but I'm staying home."

There was another loud silence. Finally Dad shook his head. "This is how it's got to be, kiddo. Anyway, I know you'll love camp. It'll be a terrific experience."

I'd love being shipped off to some camp I'd never heard of? When pigs could fly!

"What it will be is very expensive," I said, trying to sound logical. "I thought we were slowly going broke. How can you afford to send us to camp?"

Another loaded silence, ended by my mother.

"Your grandmother is paying for camp. You should be grateful for the opportunity. Tomorrow you can call her to say thank you."

That did it. My brain boiled over and I ran out of the room.

Chapter Three

I COULDN'T GET OUT OF bed. What was the point? I wasn't going to camp, and they weren't going to change their minds.

Mom and Dad—I wish I could find something else to call them—had become strangers. How could all this have happened without my noticing? Was I blind? Stupid? Maybe they were both just really good actors. Liars, more like it. Traitors, even. We'd trusted them, and look what they'd done.

They took turns bringing me trays of stuff I couldn't eat. I buried my face in the pillow and prayed for sleep.

On the second day someone knocked so softly I almost didn't hear it. Maybe Sally had come to see if I was still alive.

"Who is it?" I croaked.

"It's me."

The whispered answer didn't help much.

"Which me?"

The door opened and shut without a sound, and Jeremy tiptoed into the room. I could smell his particular mix of bicycle grease and sweat.

He sat down on the edge of my bed.

I started to cry again, stuffing my face back into the soggy pillow.

He picked up the hand nearest to him and gently unwound my fingers from their fist. He put something hard and twiggy into my palm and closed my fingers over it.

"I'm sorry, kid," he said. "I'll try to figure something out."

He turned away, closed the door, and was gone.

I sat up and leaned against the wall. One of my horses, maybe the sole surviving member of my herd, lay cradled in my hand. It was the Belgian mare, blonde and enormous, hairy feet and all. The foal that used to follow at her foot had broken off and was gone.

Tears dripped and joined the river of snot running down my face. I wiped it with a corner of the sheet, tucked the mare safely under my pillow, and went back to sleep.

I WOKE UP TO DAD standing near the bed with his arms full of clean linen. My world was ending and he wanted to change the sheets? I turned back to my pillow but he sat down, put his arms around me, and pulled me onto his lap.

"We'll get through this, kiddo. I'm not sure how, but we'll get through it."

I rubbed my face against his shoulder. Dad was the one who always understood me. When Mom and Jeremy thought I was terminally weird, he would translate for them. How could he have let this happen?

He stood up and put me down in my room's one comfy chair. Then, quick as a flash, he stripped off the bedding, threw my soaking pillow on the pile, and remade the bed. My Belgian landed on the carpet, luckily unhurt. I grabbed her before Dad could step on her.

"I see that you're upset," he said.

Upset? Pul-eeze!

"And I understand why you don't want to go to camp."

I waited.

"What about a camp with horses? Don't they have camps where kids ride every day? Wouldn't that be fun?"

Okay, I thought. That's the carrot. Where's the stick?

"It was Jeremy's idea."

Had someone kidnapped my brother and left a copy in his place?

"Your mother is asking around about horse camps. Maybe she can find something that fills the bill."

He paced around the room like a caged bear.

"I know it seems like we don't care how you and Jeremy feel. I understand you want to stay home this summer. Maybe you even think you can fix things, make your mother and me go back to how we were before."

He was quiet.

"The truth is, we haven't been happy together for a long, long time. Some things can't be fixed, and our marriage is one of them."

I put my hands over my ears and yelled over his words.

"You could! If you really wanted, you could make it better!"

Tears started dripping again. "Don't you care about us at all?"

He just stood there, saying nothing. I lay back down on my bed, face in the cool dry pillow, waiting for a miracle.

Dad left the room, gently closing the door behind him.

MOM BROUGHT LUNCH ON A tray. Chicken noodle soup and buttered toast cut into triangles. She'd even cut the crusts off.

The smell made me gag.

Supper was macaroni and cheese, my favorite. I couldn't even look at it.

Pulling the covers over my head, I went back to sleep.

When I woke up my mouth was full of cotton wool, and I was dying of thirst. I crawled out of bed and went to the kitchen for water.

A pamphlet lay on the counter near the sink. Under a picture of girls riding down a dirt road in the woods were the words "Secret Lake Camp, Fairlee, Vermont."

I opened it. Pictures of girls riding horses over fences, grooming horses, even one of a girl kissing her horse on the nose. A mountain lake with girls canoeing and sailing. A cabin full of smiling girls in pajamas getting ready for bed.

It didn't look too bad. Then I read the fatal words: "Come and meet your Summer Horse."

I was hooked.

Chapter Four

THE TRAIN FROM HUDSON STOPPED at Fairlee. It was so small I couldn't find it in my *U.S. Gazetteer*, but here we were. A man with a Secret Lake sign was standing on the platform, and trunks were being deposited in a pile around him.

Ten of us got off the train. Eight strangers and Leslie and me. Leslie was pretty much a stranger, too. My mother had asked her friends about riding camps, and somebody knew someone whose daughter went to Secret Lake. That was Leslie. She was supposed to look after me on the train but, of course, she didn't. I didn't need babysitting anyway. What can happen on a train?

I found a bench near the trunks and pulled out my copy of *Black Beauty*. If I started crying I could always blame it on the book.

The last trunk arrived, and a cute teenager with a blond flattop loaded the baggage onto the camp truck. We climbed in and sat on our trunks. I kept on reading.

We'd been told to wear camp uniform on the train: white shirts with Secret Lake on the pocket, green shorts, green cardigan, and a stupid white hat like a sailor's cap with the brim turned down in front. I felt like an idiot. Nobody else seemed to mind, but I bet Leslie wouldn't have been caught dead dressing like this at home.

The truck started up, and we all had to hold on to our hats. Really.

WE DROVE THROUGH A LANDSCAPE of hilly farms and thick piney woods. After about half an hour the driver turned through a tall wooden archway. "Secret Lake Camp founded 1949" was painted across the top in green. The truck stopped in a dirt square with a flagpole at one end. An American flag flew from the top of the pole, and a dark green banner with rearing white horses facing each other flew below it.

A woman wearing the camp uniform (minus the hat) called out names and cabin numbers, and everyone went off to find their cabins.

Everyone except me.

She wore a name tag with Annette in big letters and underneath, in smaller letters, Head Counselor. She introduced herself and crossed my name off a list on her clipboard, then walked with me down a dirt path, past a few brown buildings with porches in front. I was in Cabin One, she said, pointing down the path. She gestured to a long green building about halfway along and said it was the noss.

"The what?"

"You know," Annette said. "It's where the toilets and showers are."

"Oh."

Why can't they just call it the bathroom?

Cabin One had six cots, two on each side, not counting the side with the door. Two cots had trunks at their feet; the other four had nothing but blankets, sheets, and a towel folded onto the pillow. What looked like my trunk stood under a window near the door.

"Nancy Aptow is the only one of your cabin mates to have arrived so far," Annette said. "She's a CIT this summer and will help you get settled. Make up the bunk and organize your stuff inside your trunk. You'll use that as a dresser while you're here."

A dresser? No way! Where would I put my books? My toothbrush? I walked out onto the porch. The air smelled of pine and wood smoke.

A girl with curly blond hair and freckles walked up the steps. She was taller than me, but so is just about everybody.

"Hi," she said. "I'm Nancy. I live in Darien, Connecticut. Who are you?"

"Charlene Rittenberg, Sheffield, Massachusetts. I go by Charley. Annette says you're a CIT. What's that?"

"It means I'm a Counselor in Training. It's my first day." She smiled hugely. "There are eight of us this summer. We do lots of things, but mainly we help the counselors. I'll help with the jumping classes, take out trail rides, set up campfires—all kinds of stuff that needs doing when counselors are busy. Carol has a lot of responsibilities outside the cabin, so one of my jobs is to kind of fill in for her. Like showing you around the camp."

"Is Carol our counselor?"

"She is, and she's one of the best. You'll like her." Nancy looked around the cabin, bouncing gently on the balls of her feet. "Have you been to the barn yet? I can't wait to see my summer horse!"

"Summer horse?" My heart beat faster. "Will I see mine today, too?"

"Yeah. We all will."

"Hang on a sec." I pawed through my trunk for the

carrot sticks I'd grabbed from the fridge this morning. "Okay, let's go!"

We walked past the cabins, down a grassy track through the pines. The trees disappeared into an open meadow with two riding rings and a long green barn. Fenced paddocks had a couple of horses in each, heads down eating grass.

It was a scene right out of my dreams.

NANCY LED THE WAY INTO the barn, and we stopped in front of a vertical bulletin board with a long list. Campers were grouped according to their riding experience, and each name had a horse next to it.

"I got Classic again!" Nancy said. "Thank God. He loves to jump, and he's very gentle. He's so quiet they use him for RDA."

Wondering what RDA was, I looked for my name on the list. It was at the bottom, which wasn't a surprise, seeing as how I had no experience at all. My horse's name was Firefly.

Nancy looked at the list again but didn't say anything.

"What's Firefly like?"

She glanced at me sideways and gave a shrug, like

saying yes and no at the same time.

"He's the beginners' horse," she said. "You know, somebody's mother or sister wants to go on a trail ride over Parents' Weekend? They ride Firefly. Why would they give him to you?"

My face was burning. "Well, that's what I am, I guess. I haven't ridden very much. . . ." She looked at me. "Actually, I've never ridden at all, so . . . I guess he's the right horse for me."

"Then what are you doing here? This is a riding camp! You're supposed to know how to ride!"

We stared at each other. There wasn't anything to say.

After a moment that lasted way too long, Nancy shrugged again. "Well," she said. "Let's go meet Firefly."

We walked down an aisle of stalls, looking into each one as we passed, then went through a wide doorway leading to the paddocks. She gave each one a quick once-over but didn't pause until we were halfway down the fence line. Then she stopped, put two fingers in her mouth, and whistled.

A penny-bright chestnut looked up, whinnied, and trotted over to the fence. Nancy put her arms around its neck and crooned. "Classie, baby, I've missed you so."

She drew away far enough so they could breathe into each other's nostrils.

People actually do that! I'd read about it but couldn't imagine how it was done.

"Can I borrow some carrots? I'll pay you back."

I handed her the paper bag, and she grabbed a few and held them out to the horse. He looked really happy to see them. Maybe grass can get boring.

I watched carefully as Nancy scratched his forehead and under his mane. She gave him another hug. "Bye, big guy," she whispered. "See you later." We turned away.

"That's Classic. Isn't he gorgeous?"

I nodded. He was the prettiest horse I'd ever seen. The voice in my head that comments on my stupider moments burst out laughing. Okay, okay! So he's the first horse I've ever seen close up. He didn't look much like the horses I drew in my sketchbook, but he certainly was handsome. I'd had no idea horses were so . . . solid.

We walked past more horses, and Nancy had something to say about every one of them. Way back in a corner of the last paddock, a large white horse was rolling in the dust.

"Hey, Firefly!" Nancy yelled.

He got to his feet and shook like a dog, then looked in our direction. Dismissing us, he turned his back and wandered over to the paddock's only tree. He stood in the shade, resting his weight on one hind foot, and went to sleep.

My eyes filled with disappointed tears.

I rubbed my eyes and sneezed. Nancy took a deep breath and ducked under the fence. "Watch out for the top rail," she said. "It's hot."

I examined it carefully. The top rail looked just like the other two.

"It's electrified," she explained. "If you touch the wire you could get zapped."

I squeezed under the middle rail, staying as far away from the top one as I could.

"Come on." Nancy walked purposefully across the field.

We stopped five or six feet away from Firefly. Close up, he was more gray than white. He had reddish marks like big pimples all over his body. His mane and tail were brown with dust and twigs.

"Why's he that funny color?" I asked. "Has he been sick?"

Nancy laughed. "No, that's how he's supposed to

look. It's a color called flea-bitten gray. I kind of like it. It's different."

So this was my summer horse. He wasn't a pony, that's for sure. My head barely came up to his withers.

I got this from *Complete Horse and Pony Care*: If you want to know how tall a horse is, measure from the top of the big bump at the low end of his neck—his withers—to the ground. Every four inches is a "hand." My hands aren't four inches across, even if you count my thumbs, but however many hands high Firefly was, that's how high I am, too.

Maybe, I thought, he likes carrot sticks. I dug into the bag and grabbed a handful. As soon as Firefly caught a whiff, his head came up. All of a sudden I was interesting. He chomped the carrots up in one big mouthful and orange slobber dripped off his chin. Then he walked closer and rubbed his carrot-y muzzle all over my white camp shirt, paying particular attention to the pockets.

I reached up to give his forehead a scratch. If Classic liked it, maybe Firefly would, too. He didn't comment, but he didn't move away, either. I thought about trying the breathe-in-his-nostrils thing but couldn't make myself do it.

I laughed. Just being near Firefly was cheering me

up. A real live horse! So what if he was old and looked like he had the chicken pox? Maybe camp wasn't going to be so bad after all.

Chapter Five

AFTER GIVING FIREFLY THE REST of the carrots, Nancy and I took the long way back to the cabin. We passed the dining hall, the arts and crafts hut, and the noss.

"Why's it called that?" I asked. Nancy looked mysterious but didn't answer. "Is it okay to stop here? I really need to pee."

After, as I washed my hands, I stood on tiptoe to look in the mirror over the sink. Blah-brown hair, turning under at the tips. Straight-cut bangs, partway hidden by my stupid hat. Dark eyebrows trying their best to meet over my nose. So much had happened you'd think I'd look different, but I was just the same.

"The showers are over there." Nancy pointed to a doorway leading to another room. "If you want hot water, you'd better get here early."

Back outside, Nancy pointed her chin towards a small log building with a wrap-around porch. "It's the office. We have assembly and flag-raising out front every morning. If you get a package or need to call home, that's where you go. Our mailboxes are on the porch. Mail comes twice every day but only once on Saturday. Sunday it doesn't come at all."

Mail. My eyes filled up again. I already felt desperate for news from home. Where was Dad? Had he moved out for good? I thought about Jeremy, too. He was at a boys' camp somewhere on the lake. He'd left a few days before me. I wondered how he was doing, but even if he was dying he'd never let me know. And Mom. All alone in our big house. I knew she was coping—she and Jeremy always coped—but I couldn't imagine how it felt to be completely on her own.

Well, I thought, she made her choice. I refuse to feel sorry for her.

"Coming?" Nancy shifted her weight from foot to foot, ready to be off. "You want to see the waterfront or go back to the cabin and make your bed?" It wasn't hard to know which one she wanted.

"Let's see where we swim. And maybe where we canoe?" I love canoeing. It's one sport I'm good at.

"Sure. We'll go behind the office and follow the trail to the lake."

Another group of campers was getting out of the truck. You could tell the new kids by how lost they looked in their ridiculous hats. The old-timers had worked out how to make the hats look kind of cute. None of them, I noticed, had bangs.

THE TRAIL TO SECRET LAKE went through the woods, joined by other trails that probably led from the cabins. I could smell the lake before I saw it: that green, cold, fishy smell I love.

The waterfront was an H-shaped dock with diving boards on one side and a platform on the other. Beyond the dock was a raft for horsing around. We cruised past the canoe dock but didn't stop. Apart from three canoe racks filled with boats, there wasn't much to see.

We headed back to the cabin. "I wonder who's bunking in with us," Nancy said, picking up the pace. "Maybe there'll be another first-timer and you can learn the ropes together." She stared dreamily into space. "My first summer here there were three of us new campers in my cabin. Did we ever have a blast! We didn't get thrown out . . . but we were warned."

"What did you do?" I couldn't imagine.

"Well, for one thing, we insisted on wearing our camp hats the whole summer. Soon, half the kids were wearing them, too. Then we stopped. We took bets to see how long it would take for everyone to stop." She smiled. "Longer than you might think. Then there was the mysterious rash of short-sheeted beds. . . ." Nancy giggled. "We're lucky they let us come back!"

We walked up the steps and stopped on the porch. My heart started to race and my mouth went dry as dry. I wanted to see who else was in the cabin but, at the same time, not so much. What is it Dad always says? "Ignorance is bliss"? So long as I didn't know, I could imagine living with four best friends for the summer. Five, counting Nancy. We climbed the steps to the porch, and I forced myself to open the door.

A girl was kneeling in front of my open trunk. Two others looked over her shoulder at my sketchbook.

"Hey, look at this! She uses the *You Can Draw Horses* book. I stopped copying that when I was eight."

Nancy pushed past me. "Hey! Jane! Put that back! What do you think you're doing?" She was on fire.

Jane ignored Nancy and got to her feet. She could have won the prize for medium: medium height; medium weight; medium brown hair cut medium short. The only thing that wasn't medium was the look on her face. It was one hundred percent nasty.

Nancy shoved her face right into Jane's and grabbed the sketchbook.

"I don't know what you think you're doing," she growled, "but in this cabin we don't snoop in other peoples' trunks. Apologize! Now!"

Jane wandered over to a bunk on the opposite wall and sat down. The other two just stood there, looking embarrassed.

"How come your summer horse is Firefly?" Jane sneered. "He's only for babies who don't know how to ride."

My throat closed up. Nancy answered for me. "None of your business. Are you going to act like a Secret Lake camper, or would you like to take a walk while Charley meets the girls she's going to live with this summer?"

Jane's face turned a blotchy red. She thumped down on her bunk and sulked. Nancy turned her back on Jane and moved in front of the two girls who'd been looking at my sketchpad. One was tall and thin with straight blond hair and a bad case of sunburned nose. The other was short with curly black hair, glasses, and more than her share of baby fat.

"This is Charlene Rittenberg," Nancy announced, "but she goes by Charley. It's her first time at camp, and I'm showing her the ropes. Charley, the one with the curls is Debbie Taylor, and this is Pam Carr. They live in Mount Kisco, New York and have been riding together for a couple of years. I don't know what's gotten into them. They're usually pretty nice."

Pam and Debbie muttered something that sounded like "Sorry," and "Nice to meet you," and sat down on their bunks. I managed to smile, but it probably looked like I was making faces. Everything I had went into trying not to cry.

"And who are you?" Nancy smiled at a large girl with glasses and long dark hair held back with a plastic hairband. She sat on her bunk looking like she wanted to disappear.

"My name is Evelyn. Evie. Evie Krull." Her voice was so quiet we could hardly hear it. She cleared her throat. "I live in New Jersey. My parents drove me."

The cabin door opened.

"Hi, Carol," called Nancy. She turned to the rest of us. "Carol's our counselor this summer, which is pretty lucky for us."

"And Nancy is our CIT for the summer," Carol said, "which is pretty lucky for her!"

She stood in the doorway and looked us over, hands on hips. I looked her over back. She was tall, like Nancy, with dark brown hair pulled into a long, high ponytail and the longest legs I'd ever seen. She was . . . beautiful.

"I see you're all here and starting to get acquainted."

She frowned at Jane. "At the Welcome Dinner tonight you'll hear about what's happening this summer, and the food will be great. In the meantime make your beds and clean yourselves up. Stay in uniform. That's white shirt, green shorts, white socks. And bring your cardigans. It can get chilly once the sun goes down. Any questions?"

Evie held up her hand with the little white hat swinging from one finger. She looked a question at Carol.

"No hats," Carol said. "You only have to wear them when you travel."

"Are we allowed to wear shoes?" asked Jane from her corner. Pam and Debbie laughed, Evie looked blank, and Nancy ignored her.

Carol winked and left the cabin.

"Whew," said Nancy. "That was lucky. If she'd come a few minutes earlier, there'd have been trouble. Carol's a terrific counselor. My sister had her a couple of summers ago and loved her. She's a lot of fun and she knows everything about horses. But she can't stand bullies."

She threw Jane a look. Jane looked away.

"Okay, then. Evie and Charley, grab your soap and towels and follow me."

Chapter Six

WE HEADED TO THE WELCOME Dinner as a cabin. Jane took her own sweet time getting ready, so we were late leaving. I walked with Evie, who looked about as overwhelmed as I felt.

The dining hall was set up for a party. Round tables, each with a white tablecloth and vase of wildflowers, filled the room. At the front a long narrow table faced the campers. Annette sat there, along with some other people who were probably the instructors, or whatever you call them at camp.

When everyone was settled, someone tapped her glass with a knife and the room quieted down. The glass-tapper stood up.

"Welcome to Secret Lake Camp," she said. Her voice was clear and loud enough to be heard all over the room. "My name is Lisa Behrens, and this is a very special night for me. Tonight begins the tenth summer since Secret Lake was founded by my grandmother, and my fourth summer in charge. With your help and enthusiasm, we can make this the best summer ever."

I looked her over carefully. She was middle-sized and a little plump, with straight brown hair cut short and an open, friendly face. It was hard to believe she'd run the camp for four years. She looked too young and somehow unused.

"I see many familiar faces and a few newcomers to Secret Lake. A very hearty welcome to all. Tonight I'll introduce our staff and give you a preview of how the summer will go. But first things first. It's time to eat. Tonight's special meal will be served by your counselors. This doesn't happen often, so enjoy it. But first, let's join hands and sing 'Friends.' Many of you know how we do it here, so give the new campers a little help."

We all held hands and started to sing: "Make new friends, but keep the old. One is silver, and the other gold." The group split into three and sang it as a round. I know the song, so that was okay. I was just glad not to have to hold hands with Jane.

It was a wonderful meal. It started with fruit cocktail and ended with the main course: steak or chicken, and baked potatoes with butter, sour cream and chives. You could choose green beans or a salad. No dessert. That was a relief. I was too full to eat another bite.

When the tables were cleared, Lisa Behrens stood up again. She introduced five riding instructors, two for Swimming, two for Arts and Crafts, and one for Canoeing and Sailing. Archery, Riflery, and Drama each had its own instructor. There were a bunch of others, but my stomach was full. It was hard to keep my eyes open.

Then it was Annette's turn. "Alright, campers, please follow me!"

I woke up fast. Where were we going?

It doesn't get all-the-way dark in June until about nine o'clock, but the sun was nearly down. Annette led the way along a path through the woods. Fireflies were starting to spark, and I couldn't help thinking about Firefly, my summer horse. Maybe tomorrow I'd have my first lesson. The fireflies moved into my chest and did a little dance.

We stopped in a clearing with pine trees all around and the makings of a fire in the middle. Numbered strips of green carpet were laid in rows around the fireplace. Mrs. Behrens walked to the middle of the circle. "Sit down, everyone, cabin by cabin."

The crowd of campers muddled around until everyone was sitting. Cabin One was close to the fire pit. It was a tight squeeze to fit us all on the rug, but I wriggled in between Evie and Nancy, as far away from Jane as I could get.

Mrs. Behrens waited until we were quiet. "It's time to talk about what this camp is all about.

"The easy answer is 'horses.' And so it is. But in a more important way it's about friendship, about meeting new people and learning new skills.

"Many of you are used to having your parents, or maybe an older sister or brother, looking out for you. Here at Secret Lake you have counselors and staff doing their best to keep everyone happy, but there's a lot they don't see. You have to look out for one another. That way small problems stay small. When they're small, we can fix them."

I glanced at Nancy, thinking about how she'd looked after me since I first got to the cabin. She didn't understand how or why I was at camp, but she tried hard to help. And she defended me when Jane invaded my trunk. Even though she hardly knew me, she'd been a real friend. Maybe it was part of that CIT thing, but I was grateful.

"We have lots of activities at camp this summer," Mrs. Behrens continued, "more than ever before. Some you can pick; some are not optional. We want you to go home in August having done things you would never choose on your own. We want you to grow, in confidence and in knowledge. We want you to look back on this summer with pride in your own achievements.

"Every week we have a campfire. We sing and eat and make s'mores. Someone gives a little talk at every campfire. A talk to make you laugh, or cry, or learn a lesson. At the last campfire of the summer everyone writes a 'Letter to Self.'

"I write one, as do all the staff. We write about what we've learned, about our triumphs, and about our troubles, too. Campers who've been here before look at their letters from previous years. They can see how far they've come since they started."

She struck a match and set the flame to the crushed newspaper and kindling. The wood caught fire and a campfire blossomed in the darkness.

"And now," she said, "it's time to stop talking and have dessert."

Chapter Seven

THE WALK BACK TO THE cabin seemed very long, and all I wanted was my bed.

Tiny candles set in brown paper bags half-filled with sand lit the path. I'd heard of lights like this but had never seen one. Their soft glow and the delirious fireflies turned the woods into fairyland.

"What do you think, Evie?" I asked. "Is camp going to be okay? Have you ever been to a sleep-away camp before?"

"I went to one last year," Evie said softly. "It was very snooty, and I didn't fit in. I hope this summer is better."

"What did you think when Jane opened my trunk?"

"I thought it was hers." Evie stared at the path in front of her feet. "I'm sorry she did it. She was horrible."

"Yeah. I wonder if she's always like this, looking for someone to pick on." I gave myself a shake. "Well, she's not going to pick on me. The only thing to do is ignore her. Bullies can't stand being ignored."

Evie didn't answer, but that was okay. We walked the rest of the way in friendly silence.

The lights in the cabin were on. Everyone was back, but no one was in pj's yet. Carol was reading from a clipboard and talking about the plan for tomorrow. I sat on my bunk and listened.

The weekly activity schedule was posted on the boards in every cabin, but riding class assignments would keep changing until everyone was in the right class. She read out the assignments for tomorrow.

Nancy was in the advanced group and would help out with the intermediate jumping classes.

Pam and Debbie had just moved into the intermediates but were in different classes. Carol told them when their lessons would be, and named their instructors. Pam made a face, and Debbie bounced angrily on her bunk.

"But we always ride together!" she burst out. "Can't you change it?"

Carol looked at them for a moment and made a note on her clipboard. "I'll check it out, but I can't promise."

She carried on with assignments. Evie and Jane were with the beginners, but Carol was quick to say it didn't mean they couldn't ride. They just needed a little more work on the basics—whatever those were. Jane looked like she wanted to say something. Her face turned red and her jaw stuck out, but she kept her mouth shut.

I wondered how many beginner riders there were at Secret Lake. I wondered what being a beginner rider meant. I wondered what I would have to do to get sent home.

Carol looked at me. "And then there's our little anomaly."

I didn't like "little" and I didn't know what "anomaly" meant, but I probably wouldn't like that either.

"Do you girls remember Maria San Angelo?"

Nancy nodded, Pam and Debbie had lost interest, and Jane continued to sulk.

"She was supposed to be back this year, but three weeks ago she fell and broke her ankle. That left a hole in our roster of campers, one we didn't know how to fill. Then Charley came along."

Five pairs of eyes were suddenly riveted on me.

"She wanted to spend the summer at a riding camp. Her parents were willing, but neither they nor Charley knew much about finding a good one. Leslie McIntosh, a senior in Cabin Seven who lives in their town, recommended Secret Lake. And *voila*! Here she is.

"I call her an anomaly because she is unique in the history of Secret Lake. Charley doesn't know how to ride. Yet. We have plans to change that in a hurry.

"I expect all of you"—she looked at Jane—"ALL of you, to make her feel welcome and help in any way you can. Lois, our chief instructor, has made teaching Charley her summer project, and I have no doubt she'll join a beginners' class very soon."

All my good feelings from the Welcome Dinner disappeared. I felt like a bug under a microscope.

Carol glanced at her clipboard. "Charley, you'll meet with Lois at the barn right after breakfast. Please wear jodhpurs and boots. And don't look so shattered. It'll be fun.

"All right, girls, that's it for tonight. Time to get ready for bed. Lights out in twenty minutes."

Carol turned and left the cabin, and everybody started talking at once.

I picked up my toilet bag and towel, then grabbed my pajamas and headed for the noss. No way was I getting undressed in front of Jane.

I heard footsteps behind me on the path. I didn't turn around, but the hairs on the back of my neck were prickling. A hand touched my arm, and I flinched.

"It's only me," came a whisper near my left shoulder.

I stopped short and Evie bumped into my back.

"I thought you might like some company," she said. "And, anyway, I don't remember where the bathroom is."

Chapter Eight

I WAS TOO EXCITED TO sleep. My first riding lesson was in the morning, and I couldn't keep my eyes shut.

Tomorrow I'd be riding! What would it be like? Would Firefly remember me? Maybe I should bring the carrot sticks. No. Firefly finished them off. Or maybe an apple? Where could I find an apple?

He's awfully tall. How will I get on? The ponies in my books are all, well, ponies. They're small. Firefly is big. I'll probably need a ladder. I don't like heights, but maybe it won't matter. He *has* to like me! He's my summer horse!

My thoughts spun as I sank down into sleep. Then I was riding bareback down the Chincoteague beach, afraid of nothing, free as the wind.

I slept through reveille and spent so much time getting into my riding clothes that everyone was at breakfast before I was dressed. It didn't matter. I was too excited to eat.

When I got to the barn, Firefly was tied in the aisle

waiting for his day to start. I said hi and reached up to stroke his neck. He ignored me. Not even a sniff to see if I had carrots.

He was covered with dust and twigs were caught in his mane. I worked my fingers through the tangles and gently removed all the sticks I could reach. A bucket against the wall was full of brushes and stuff to groom a horse. I picked up a brush and ran it gently over Firefly's back.

"First you have to loosen the dirt." A tall thin woman with pixie-cut red hair and pale delicate-looking skin walked over to Firefly. She handed me a flat rubber something with a place to stick my hand and a rim like the edge of a piecrust. "It's a currycomb," she said. "You rub it in circles and the dirt comes to the surface. Then you can brush it off."

She showed me how to do it, and Firefly's coat turned brown where the comb had been. Why, I wondered, do they call it a comb?

"Now you try," she said. I tried, but not much dirt came up. "Lean into it. Grooming a horse requires muscle."

Firefly looked bored, but he didn't seem to mind. I kept trying to get the dirt up.

"My name is Lois, and I'm going to give you your

lesson today. When we see how you ride, I'll decide where you belong."

See how I ride? Was she the only person in the camp who wasn't in on the secret?

My arm ached, and I was getting a stiff neck from looking up. I dropped the currycomb back in the bucket. Lois picked it up and kept on rubbing. When she reached his back, Firefly wiggled, and I jumped out of the way.

"What's he doing? Doesn't he like it?" I knew I sounded panicky, and I took a deep breath.

"He's just a bit ticklish. We have to make sure to get his back clean. Even a little grit can cause a saddle sore."

Next she handed me a brush with stiff bristles about two inches long. "This is a dandy brush," she said. "We use it to remove the dirt we've brought to the surface. At the end of each stroke give a little flick—like this— to get the dirt out of the brush."

The brush was big for my hand and made me feel clumsy, but I gave it a flick. The dirt came out of the brush, smack into my face. I rubbed my eyes with both hands, feeling like an idiot, and Lois laughed.

I glared at her.

"Sorry," she said quickly. "I was just remembering

the first time I tried to groom a horse. I stepped back into the bucket and fell over. The horse jumped, I screamed, and everything went downhill from there."

She traded the dandy brush for a smaller brush with soft bristles. "This is a body brush. We use it last. It gets rid of whatever dust is left, and the horse likes it." Firefly's back relaxed as I brushed where the dandy brush had been. He closed his eyes and his lower lip hung down.

Lois tidied his mane and tail with a wide-toothed comb, and he was done.

Whoops. Not quite. She took a metal hook from the bucket and ran her hand down a back leg. Firefly picked up his hoof, and Lois poked around in it. She checked all four feet.

"You don't want him to work with stones in his hoof. Even a pebble could make him lame."

I knew that. I'd read all about it. How could I have forgotten about picking out his feet?

"Firefly's saddle is over there." Lois pointed. "Please find it and bring it to me"

A row of saddles sat on racks against the wall, each one with a bridle hanging below it from a hook. Little white labels on every rack had horses' names inked on. I found Firefly's and pulled it down. It weighed a ton.

It had its own pad, so I brought that too.

Lois took the saddle and looked at me. "You want to try and put it on? The pad goes first. Put it over his withers and slide it down so the hair's all going the same way."

I got the pad on, but the saddle was beyond me. Firefly was just too tall. Lois brought over a set of portable steps. "Try standing on the mounting block."

It was hard to climb the block's three steps carrying the saddle, but I managed to heave it up onto his back. Just. Lois caught it before it slipped over the other side.

"That's enough for this morning. I'll finish tacking him up. Have some breakfast." She handed me three oatmeal cookies wrapped in a napkin and a carton of chocolate milk.

FIREFLY WAS READY IN TWO minutes flat. Lois held out a couple of velvet-covered helmets. "Pick the one that fits best. It's your first lesson, and we don't want to take anything for granted."

Did she think I was going to fall off?

Lois picked up Firefly's halter and put it on over the bridle. Then she clipped on a lead rope and handed it to me. "Lead him out to the ring, why don't you? Just go through that door and turn left. The gate is open."

My heart started to bang against my ribs. I was going to lead a horse for the first time!

I went to his left side and took a few steps. Firefly just stood there. I tugged on the rope, and he braced his feet. I moved in front of him, turned to face him, and really pulled. He put his ears back and stayed put. Why wouldn't he walk?

Lois took the rope. "Try it like this." She stood next to him, clucked with her tongue, and said "Walk up." He walked a few steps and then stopped when she said "Whoa."

She handed me the lead rope. "Now you try it." I did, and Firefly walked nicely to the door and out into the sunshine. I was so excited I forgot to be embarrassed.

Pam, Debbie, and Jane were standing by the fence.

I stopped walking but Firefly kept on going. And going.

"Say whoa," Lois said softly. "Just speak to him and he'll stop."

"Whoa!" I yelled.

Firefly turned his head and gave me a dirty look, but he stopped.

"Can I help you girls with anything?" Lois asked.

"No? Good. There are stalls to be picked out and horses to groom. If you've any extra time, the saddle soap. . . ."

Jane and her buddies disappeared.

"Let's see how long your stirrups need to be. Stand facing Firefly's side. Now pick up a stirrup, put it right up into your armpit, and stretch out your arm."

I rolled my eyes. She was kidding, right?

"No. I mean it. See how much too long the leathers are? That's how much we have to shorten them. They need to be as long as your arm with your fingers stretched out."

She moved the buckle up four holes and checked the length again, then moved around the horse and shortened the other one.

"Only one thing left to do," Lois said. "Can you guess?"

No idea. I kept my mouth shut and shook my head. Lois put her hand between Firefly's stomach and the wide leather band that went around his belly. "Is the girth tight enough?" She made a fist in the gap. I shook my head again.

"Many horses hate having the girth tightened. They swallow air and blow out their stomachs. If you wait a few minutes and check again, you'll often find that the girth is loose."

She pulled up the girth slowly, tightening it one hole at a time. "This guy's a master at blowing out. You always have to check. Okay, Charley, lead Firefly to the mounting block."

I took a deep breath, stood next to Firefly's head and said, "Walk up." He walked over to the mounting block like a little lamb. This time I remembered to say whoa.

"Well done. Now lead him behind the block until he's standing alongside it, and say whoa again."

I did, and he did.

"Good. Now you are going to Mount This Horse." I could hear the capital letters. "First, step onto the mounting block.

"Face the saddle and pick up the reins with your left hand." She helped me untangle the reins and showed me how to hold them.

"Hold onto the saddle with your right hand, and with your left, grab a big hunk of Firefly's mane, as close to the skin as you can."

I gave her a look. If I grabbed his mane Firefly might bite me.

"No, Charley, I mean it. Grab his mane. I promise it won't hurt him—and it'll anchor the hand holding the reins so you don't jab him in the mouth."

I had to lean over to reach the mane, but Lois was right. He didn't seem to care.

"Now put your left foot in the stirrup. I've got the lead rope. He won't go anywhere."

As soon as I picked up my left foot, Firefly stepped away from the block and I had to let go. I looked at Lois.

"Okay, horses do that sometimes. Step down and lead him around again."

I took the lead rope and lined him up next to the block. "Up you get," said Lois. I got up and tried again but, as soon as my foot got close to the stirrup, Firefly stepped away.

Someone giggled behind the bushes.

I kept trying to get my foot into the stirrup, and Firefly kept edging away. Lois didn't give up, so I couldn't either. Firefly clearly thought this was great fun.

After playing the game for what felt like an hour, I couldn't tell my right foot from my left. I didn't know what to put where, and I didn't feel safe enough to try. Maybe carrots would have helped, but I was done for today.

I stepped down from the mounting block, handed

the reins to Lois, and walked out of the ring. As soon as I turned the corner, I ran.

I was crying too hard to look where I was going and ran right past the cabins into the woods.

Chapter Nine

IT WASN'T MUCH OF A woods. In two minutes I was out the other side in a meadow full of wildflowers. Nice. I picked one—it looked a little like a daisy but didn't have a daisy's prickly scent. I found a tree and sat in the shade, wishing I'd brought a Musketeers bar or something. My barn breakfast was far in the past.

I was making a list in my head of everything I hated about horse camp when I heard something. It sounded like a nicker, or maybe a little whinny.

A small black horse stretched his head over the bars of a split-rail fence. He nickered again, like he was calling me. Come on! I thought. This isn't happening! My stomach hurt with wanting him to be real.

He arched his neck, tossed his head, and stamped a front hoof. I stood up and walked over to the fence.

He stood up against the bars, swishing his tail and staring at me. I moved closer until we stood nose to nose. He puffed out some air and stood waiting. I waited too. Another big puff. Another wait. Was he doing that Classic thing? Was I supposed to do what

Nancy did?

Feeling stupid, and very glad no one was watching, I blew into his nose. He sighed loudly and dropped his head down to the grass.

I watched him graze for a long time. Did you know horses have beautiful eyelashes? His were like tiny black wires. I wanted to go under the fence for a closer look, but someone was calling my name, and I knew I had to get back.

Carol walked into the meadow. "Who's this cutie?" she asked.

Her choice of words ticked me off. He wasn't "cute." He was gorgeous!

I turned around to say goodbye, but he was moving away towards the back fence. If he could keep a secret, I guess I could, too.

I floated back to the cabin. That horse was real. He wanted to know me. He stamped his foot to make me walk over to meet him. He breathed into my nose!

Not even lunch with Jane could ruin that.

As it turned out, I didn't have to sit with Jane. Campers eat lunch wherever they want. I sat with Evie and a girl I hadn't met whose name was Birdie. She was in Cabin Three and the only black camper at Secret Lake.

I wondered if she felt as out of place as I did.

Chapter Ten

I DREADED GOING BACK TO the cabin. How many of those snickers had come from girls I had to eat, sleep, and everything else with for the next eight weeks?

I walked past the archery range (empty), the swimming area (full of older girls practicing what looked like life saving), and the arts and crafts hut. I watched campers chatting away, braiding, weaving, and modeling various useless objects and felt like a freak.

I walked up the cabin steps, took a deep breath and opened the door. Five pairs of eyes looked up, then back down.

"Hi, Charley," Nancy said. "How'd it go?"

"Yeah, Charley, did you ever actually sit on the horse?"

Instead of listening, I concentrated on memorizing names: Evie Krull, Jane Blake, Debbie Something. . . .

I knew what they were all thinking: that I was a loser with a capital L.

"Knock it off," said Nancy. "We all had to start

somewhere, and it probably wasn't pretty."

"Maybe it wasn't," Jane said. "But at least I got into the saddle."

"You and how much help?"

Nancy didn't wait for Jane to answer. "I started lessons when I was six, fat and clumsy and scared to death. My big sister was the horse star in the family, and she leaned over the fence laughing her head off. I couldn't quite get my foot into the stirrup, and the pony kept edging away just the tiniest bit, with me hopping on one leg after him. I was in tears by the time Dad picked me up and plopped me into the saddle."

Memories of first rides flooded the cabin. Everybody had a story. By the time the activity bugle blew again, they'd forgotten I was even there.

That was fine by me.

The truth was it didn't matter so much anymore. My whole world had changed. I might be the camp's laughing stock. I might be the only one in the history of the world to go to horse camp without knowing how to ride. I might not be able to get my butt into the saddle without a crane. But I had something none of them had. I had that friendly black horse on my side.

I couldn't wait to see him again.

Chapter Eleven

Dear Sally,

So far, camp has been awful. I'm in a cabin with five other girls, but only two of them even speak to me. Maybe they're afraid what I have is catching. They'll wake up in the morning and won't know how to ride, just like me.

There's this girl in my cabin. Jane Blake. She was pawing through my trunk when I walked in and went out of her way to be nasty. I can tell she's going to make my life a misery, but I don't know why. Her two buddies stand behind her like bodyguards and don't say a word. It's creepy.

I really hate it here. The kids have no manners. They whisper behind my back. Is it because I don't know how to ride? I wish they'd just mind their own business and leave me alone. And nobody reads! I feel like a visitor from another planet—a planet where everybody loves books and no one wants to weave potholders.

The horses aren't what I expected either. I get it that they're big, but I thought they'd be friendly. Mine won't even look me in the eye. He's an ugly grayish horse with red mosquito-bite-looking spots all over and a stringy gray mane. His feet are enormous, and I'm always afraid he's going to step on me.

If I could lift his saddle up, I'd need a ladder to put it on his back, and he always blows his belly out when I try to tighten the girth. My instructor lets me help tack him up, but we both know I can't do it.

I can't seem to do anything right. In my first lesson I couldn't even get into the saddle. Jane and her sidekicks watched from the bushes and laughed at me. It was humiliating.

It hasn't been all bad, though. I met this funny little black horse yesterday. He came over to the fence and breathed in my face. He has a wavy mane and a beautiful long tail that he lifts up when he trots. He likes me. Too bad he isn't my summer horse.

I miss you and wish I was home. Please write back.

Charley

Chapter Twelve

I COULDN'T STOP THINKING ABOUT that horse. Who was he? Who owned him? Why was he off by himself? I told the arts and crafts counselor I had a headache and went looking for him.

The field was empty.

I'd had a vision of him galloping up in a cloud of dust, showing how glad he was to see me. I walked along the fence, hoping he'd appear. After my disaster with Firefly I needed to get my dreams back. This horse would be different. I could feel it.

Where was he hiding? I looked everywhere, behind the bushes growing against the fence, under the big maple, even in the woods. Maybe he wasn't anywhere. Maybe I'd made him up.

The bugle sounded for swimming and I ran back to the cabin to change. It's one thing to miss lanyard braiding. Swimming is something else again. At least it's something I know how to do. All those years of lessons might finally pay off.

After supper I went back to the paddock. He was standing under his tree, swishing away the last flies of the day. Now everything was going to be all right.

Or maybe it wouldn't. Maybe he wouldn't like me any more than Firefly did.

His head came up and his nostrils opened wide, like he was sniffing to see where I was. Then he tossed his head and neighed, really loud. I didn't know if he was happy to see me or mad, but there wasn't any time to worry about it. He galloped over to the fence and stood in front of me, snorting.

Was that a good thing? I had no idea. He came up close and started sniffing me as far as his nose could reach over the fence. I froze. If I moved too fast maybe he'd run away.

He didn't run anywhere, just stood staring at me, making little blowing sounds. I leaned over the fence and offered him my face. If he bit off my nose, Mom would kill me.

He blew into my nostrils just like before. I blew back into his, and he stepped back and tossed his head.

Come on in, he was saying. *Come on in and stay a while.*

I knew it was crazy, but I ducked under the top rail. He just stood there. I walked up to him and stopped, waiting for him to make a move. He started sniffing me again and, by the time he was done, I wasn't nervous anymore. I ran my finger through the tangles in his mane and leaned against his neck.

I had come to where I wanted to be, more than any place in the world.

We stood like that forever, then I went to the tree and leaned against it. My knees were shaking. I slid down the trunk and sat down.

He came over and dropped his head, practically into my lap. Good thing he was small, for a horse.

"Hi," I said. "What are you doing here all alone?" He snuffled my hair. "My name is Charlene. Charley for short. Pretty dumb, huh? It's because I love horses so much. You know, Charley Horse?"

He sighed, and his head dropped lower. I reached out, divided his forelock into four sections and started to braid. Yeah, I know. Braids have only three sections. When you braid a horse's mane or tail you use four, kind of like a French braid. I'd practiced at home with knitting wool.

I kept talking and braiding, taking it out and beginning again, over and over.

"My brother started it. He thought it was funny and told his friends. Pretty soon everyone was calling me

Charley Horse. After a while they dropped the horse part, but Charley stuck. I don't mind. Anything's better than *Charlene*.

"What's your name? I can't very well call you Horsie." He pushed at my hand with his nose. Back to braiding. "Don't worry, I'll think of something."

"Hey, Charley," someone called. "What are you doing here? Taps is in ten minutes, and you aren't even in your jammies."

It was Nancy, coming to find me.

"Who's this beautiful guy? He looks like a Morgan." She leaned over the fence to get a good look.

A Morgan? The black horse is a Morgan? That put the strawberry on my shortcake! I was so happy I didn't recognize myself.

Nancy cleared her throat. Loudly.

I undid the braid and stood up. "Time to go, old boy. I'll come back tomorrow."

He stood up tall, arched his neck, and trotted across the field, picking his knees up high. Then he stopped, spun around, and screamed at me, shaking his head.

"I don't think he wants you to go," said Nancy. "Sure is noisy, isn't he?"

I crawled through the fence, but I couldn't stand to leave without one more look. He whinnied again and began to graze.

I talked nonstop all the way back to the cabin. I'd made a friend! The black horse liked me! He'd let me braid his forelock. He'd sniffed my pockets—next time I'd bring an apple—and blew in my nose. I couldn't wait to see him again.

I was still talking when we got back to the cabin. Pam and Debbie gave each other that here's-the-crazy-camper look, but I didn't care. I had questions and I wanted answers.

"I need to know about the black horse," I said. Even to my ears the words came out machine-gun fast. "Who is he? Who owns him? He can't just belong to nobody."

Pam almost looked me in the eye. "I'm not sure," she said, "but I think he belongs to Mrs. Behrens' grandmother. Her name is Calhoun. Agnes, or Edith. Something like that. She still lives here, but I've never seen her."

"Nobody has," Debbie chimed in. "She's probably on the lam. Maybe she's a secret axe murderer."

"I think she died in an accident a long time ago," Nancy said.

I wasn't interested in little old ladies, especially one who abandoned the black horse and left him all alone.

"What's his name?"

Pam shrugged. "No idea."

Never mind, I promised myself. You'll figure it out.

I made a list in my head of all the things I knew:

1. He's jet black.
2. He's not very big, much smaller than Firefly.
3. He's really beautiful when he trots.
4. He yells a lot.
5. He was glad to see me.

I went to the noss to brush my teeth and everything, then got under the covers and tried to sleep. I kicked the list around in my head awhile, hoping a name would come, then played and replayed the movie of him trotting across the meadow. He looked just like a pony in a picture book.

When I woke up, it came to me: What's small, black, lively, and very noisy? A cricket!

That's his name! It's Cricket.

Chapter Thirteen

WHEN I GOT TO THE barn, Firefly was all tacked up and ready to go. I'd hoped maybe he'd remember me from yesterday, but no. He stared into the distance and acted like I wasn't there. Dreams of bonding with my summer horse crumbled a little more.

"Charley?" Lois called from the tack room. "Come find your helmet, will you? Today is going to be a big day."

A big day? The day he makes a quick side-step and dumps me on the ground?

To my surprise, the lesson started pretty well. He shuffled around while Lois checked his girth, but a growled "Stand!" made him stop fidgeting. Firefly didn't move while I fumbled with the reins. He must have spent the night standing at attention at the mounting block—it only took three tries to get into the saddle.

I wonder what she'd done to change his attitude. Whatever it was, he deserved it.

"Put some weight in your stirrups, Charley," Lois said quietly, "and keep your chin up. Your head is the heaviest part of your body, and where it goes, everything follows. Even the horse. Look where you want to go and Firefly will follow your lead."

Sure.

I tried to get my reins straight, and Lois reached up to help me. "Not so tight. We're only going for a little walk, and he won't run away."

She'd better be right. Just sitting up here was giving me the shakes. Every time I looked down I got dizzy, and the dizzier I got, the more I looked down. It felt like standing on the roof of a very tall building with no railing.

"Okay. Put your weight on your seat bones and let it flow into your feet. You want your feet to weigh a hundred pounds."

Why was she talking about my feet? I couldn't even feel them. My stomach had clenched up and I wanted to puke.

"Sit up straight and look at the letter F over there near the corner. Take a breath, let it out, and say 'Firefly, walk.'"

My body turned to stone. Everything went blurry. My first ride on a horse and I was too scared to blink!

Lois shook her head. "Let's start over," she said. "Take your feet out of the stirrups and let go of the reins. Don't worry, I've got him." She clipped a lead rope to Firefly's bridle. "Now swing your legs forward and back a few times, then let them hang down."

My foot was stuck in the stirrup. I couldn't get it out. Firefly was going to take off and I was going to be dragged! I grabbed the saddle and hung on. Firefly stretched his neck around to stare at me. Lois gently put his head back where it belonged.

"We're going to try something else. I know you're frightened, but if we stop now, you'll never be a rider." My ears pricked up. "And that will never do."

Oh, well. . . .

"You are going to stay here, on this horse, until you can ride all the way to that black letter F. I don't expect you to believe me, but you are not going to fall off."

I exhaled. Hard. Then nodded my head the tiniest bit. It was all I could manage.

What was wrong with me? I love horses and don't expect them to hurt me. Firefly is a beginner's horse! If his riders fell off all the time, they'd probably send him to the glue factory. So what if he doesn't like me? Cricket does!

I felt a warm glow in my chest. Cricket! I could do

this thing. I could do it for Cricket.

I had a sudden vision of the two horses nose to nose over a fence. Firefly was telling Cricket all about today's lesson. I'd better get it right.

". . . switch hands . . . terrific! Now put the reins on Firefly's neck, cross your arms over your chest and swing your legs again. See? Not so scary. Firefly doesn't care. He's done this a million times."

To prove her right, Firefly heaved another sigh as I gathered up the reins. What is it with horses and their sighs?

"Okay, this is a tough one. Feel around for the stirrup with your left foot and slip your toe in. Try not to touch him with your foot. Super! Now do it with your right foot."

I almost had it, but the stirrup got away and banged against Firefly's side. I grabbed the pommel, expecting the worst. He shifted his weight a little but didn't move. I tried again, and my toe slipped into the stirrup.

Got it! I felt like Sir Edmund Hillary at the top of Everest!

"Good job!" Lois tied the reins in a knot and laid them on Firefly's neck. "Hold on if you want—you won't need to steer. Just take a breath, let it out, and look over at the letter F. Say 'Firefly, walk.'"

We walked across the ring to the letter F. Then we walked back to A. Lois led Firefly all the way around the ring. I was starting to get used to the feeling of a horse moving under me. It wasn't too bad, and I felt stupid about being so scared.

Then we practiced "whoa." Every time I said it, Firefly stopped. It felt pretty good. Finally Lois untied the reins and helped me get them right. Then she unclipped the lead rope and stood out of the way. I looked at F and told Firefly to walk.

When my feet were finally back on the ground—getting off was a whole other drama—I was as limp as overcooked spaghetti. I didn't care. For the first time since leaving home, I was in control.

The noon bugle blew, and I ran to lunch. I was so hungry I could eat a. . . .

Well, maybe not. How about a pizza?

Chapter Fourteen

THE BUGLE BLEW FOR SWIMMING, releasing me from an endless hour of arts and crafts. I wondered if they'd let me bring my drawing pad and pencils. That could be the "art" in arts and crafts.

Today we were divided up into groups and swimming buddies.

I was excited about the buddy thing. I thought I might actually make a friend. But if you didn't already know someone in your group who would be your buddy, they assigned one. Guess who I got?

The only intermediate swimmer without a buddy was Jane.

The morning swim class wasn't so bad. We swam in lanes and had skills to work on, like treading water for three minutes or swimming underwater.

Free swim was going to be torture. What could Jane and I possibly do together for an hour that didn't involve talking? I found out soon enough. She jumped off the end of the dock and came up with a mouthful of gossip.

"You know Connie in Cabin Three? She's the worst rider in the whole camp. Last year she fell off fourteen times!"

Even I know that's unlikely. I kept my mouth shut and tried to block her out, but her poison kept spurting.

"Ann in Cabin Six? Her mother has been married four times, and now she's run off to Europe with a possible number five. How does Ann even remember their names?

"And that Calhoun woman, she's a real hard case. She's ridden more horses to death than you can count. I heard that black horse of yours killed her years ago. Watch out he doesn't kill you, too."

It couldn't be easy, swimming and talking at the same time, but Jane had the knack. I'll have to come up with a swim plan of my own tomorrow. Maybe I can practice breaststroke or something.

As soon as free swim was over I went looking for Cricket. A blue bucket with hoof pick, brushes, and a metal comb hung from the fence. I wondered whose stuff this was and whether it would be okay to use it.

It would have to be.

He leaned into the brushes, even the curry, and if

he'd been a cat he'd have purred. I wasn't too sure about the hoof pick, but he picked his feet up so nicely I stopped being nervous and concentrated on getting the dried mud out. I even found a small stone, maybe big enough to hurt his tender sole. How big do they have to be? Anyway, better out than in.

I put down the hoof pick and started to untangle his mane, talking all the time. Cricket was a good listener, and just being with him calmed me down. I told him about Firefly, and Jane, and how scared I am of riding.

"Isn't anybody else scared?" I asked. "No one ever talks about it. Could I be the only one?"

He didn't say anything back. Just snuffled my hair. It was enough.

It was hard to leave him to go back for supper, but I didn't want anyone to come looking. Cricket was mine, and I wanted to keep it that way.

Chapter Fifteen

MY THIRD RIDING LESSON WENT a whole lot better than the first two. Maybe I was getting used to being afraid, or maybe just getting the hang of sitting on top of a very tall, moving animal. I left the lesson feeling pretty good.

Why had mounting a horse been so hard? I can do cartwheels. I can ski. I'm not usually awkward or clumsy. So what if Firefly wasn't cooperating? His little sidesteps weren't a problem when I wasn't in a panic. Once my foot was in the stirrup, a tiny hop was all it took.

Why was I so scared? Why AM I so scared? I don't know. Except the whole horse thing is so different from what I read in books. I thought it would be personal. I thought it would be about love. I thought I would trust my horse because we had a bond.

Firefly didn't bond with me, and I couldn't make him. It made me feel—I don't know—unsafe. This is a big animal we're talking about here. With very big feet and iron shoes. He could squish me into jelly if he wanted. Not to mention those teeth!

I knew I was being stupid. Why would he want to hurt me? He's just plodding around doing his job. Squishing people isn't part of the deal.

Lois interrupted my gloomy thoughts. "Today you're going to start learning to ride."

I looked at her with my mouth hanging open.

"We're halfway through the first week. My goal is to get you and Firefly into the beginners' class as soon as possible. Maybe even as early as the end of next week."

Today was Thursday. I counted in my head. Next Friday was only eight days away. I'd only just learned to get on the horse. No way could I ride him into class in eight days. That shaky feeling I thought had gone away came back like a tidal wave.

"I can't." My voice sounded strangled.

"Sure you can," Lois said confidently. "You only have to learn a few things. Firefly can do lessons in his sleep."

What could I say that wouldn't make me sound pathetic?

"Lesson for today: steering. Take Firefly into the ring and get ready to mount up."

All by myself? Too chicken to complain out loud, I grabbed Firefly's reins and walked into the ring.

Getting on was no big deal. I checked the stirrups to make sure the length was still okay and checked the girth. After Lois pulled it a few holes tighter, I walked him around in a circle to let the saddle settle, then took him to the mounting block.

Lois stood at his head while I mounted, but she didn't have to. He stood still while I hauled myself into the saddle, put my feet in the stirrups and gathered up the reins. My hands were shaking. I hoped he couldn't tell.

"Let's get started," Lois called from the middle of the ring. "Ride him over here to me. I'm standing in the bull's eye. This is X, the dead center of the ring. I want you to ride a big circle, starting at X, with the letter A as the midpoint."

I must have looked blank because she shrugged.

"I'll walk it for you. Watch me." She trotted around the ring. "Now you do it. Follow my tracks if you want. Remember. Look where you want Firefly to go."

No matter how hard I looked, we wobbled all over the ring. Firefly's tracks looked like a drunken toddler's. Lois kept calling instructions, but I couldn't hear her. I was too nervous.

Then Firefly stumbled. I lurched forward just as his head came up. My face slammed into his neck, hard.

"Great job, Charley. That was perfect!"

Chapter Sixteen

I PULLED MYSELF UPRIGHT, BLOOD dribbling from my nose into my mouth. I wiped it off with my arm and took a deep breath. Lois looked extremely pleased with herself, and it made me mad. Instead of yelling, I started to cough.

"Sorry, sorry," Lois gasped, starting to laugh. "I know it isn't funny."

I couldn't speak.

"Listen," she said. "I've told you again and again, where your eyes go, the horse follows, right?"

I said nothing.

"Well, where were you looking?"

No answer.

"Come on, Charley, this is important. Think back. When you were walking the circle, where were your eyes?"

I mumbled something, swiping at another trickle of blood.

"What? Didn't hear you. Speak up, please."

Through gritted teeth: "At the circle. I was looking at the circle. Okay?"

She handed me a handkerchief, but by then the blood was starting to dry so it didn't do much good. Who carries handkerchiefs, anyway?

"Where was the circle, Charley? I'll answer for you. It was on the ground, right?"

So what? Can't we just get this over with so I can get off?

"You were looking at the imaginary circle on the ground, trying to follow where I walked. So where were your eyes?"

The penny dropped.

"You mean he tripped because I was looking down?"

"Bingo!

"Your head is the heaviest part of your body. When you looked down, your chin dropped. So did Firefly's. It made him lose his balance and he stumbled. I tell my students all the time to keep their chins up, not to keep them cheerful but to keep them safe. I've never seen it illustrated so graphically. I wish I could have made a movie."

I played Lois' imaginary movie in my head: Firefly tripping, me banging my face on his neck, all of it. I started to giggle. I couldn't help it. So, if my head was tilted back, his head would be too? If I craned my neck all the way around till I was looking behind me, would he walk backwards?

I laughed harder. What a great cartoon this would make!

Lois wiped her eyes. "Okay, Charley, hop off and go wash your face. Then we'll finish the lesson."

The rest of the lesson was circles, circles, and more circles. By the end, I sort of had the feel of it. Although Firefly and I still could not go around without wobbling, Lois was right. Looking where I wanted to go really helped.

We ended on a different note.

"I want you to come into the ring at A and walk a straight line to me and stop. I'll be standing at X."

I got to X, but not in a straight line. It was more like a whole bunch of S's. Circles are hard, but straight lines are murder. Still, I got there.

It wasn't perfect, but it was all mine.

I ran to the cabin and changed into my bathing suit and a T-shirt. It was time for canoeing. My nana—Dad's mother—has a summer cottage on Stockbridge Bowl, and I started canoeing as soon as I could swim.

Maybe I can't ride, but I sure know how to paddle.

Chapter Seventeen

I MADE IT TO THE dock out of breath and a little late after a sprint past Cricket's paddock. I didn't see him, but there was no time for hide and seek. Girls from all the junior cabins were at the dock, separated into their little groups. I joined the Cabin One group but might as well have been invisible.

"Listen up, campers!"

A heavy-set woman with short grayish hair stood in front of the canoe rack. There were twelve canoes and thirty campers. What were the other six supposed to do? I hoped we weren't going to have to choose partners. No one in this bunch would pick me.

"Listen up!" she said again. "My name is Gloria, and I love boats. I teach sailing and canoeing, and I hope some of you will show up in my sailing class. But, first things first. I want you to split up into two groups. If you've never been in a canoe before, line up next to me. Anyone who's had some experience with these lovely boats, you'll be in Nancy's group. Nancy, raise your hand. All of you in Nancy's group either know how to paddle or think you do. We'll have to see about that."

I walked over to Nancy, relieved that she was in the class.

"How's it going, Charley?" she asked. "I haven't seen much of you lately. Is Lois working you to the bone?"

I could feel my face turning red. "It's okay," I answered. What could I say? She'd heard kids talking. My riding lessons were daily entertainment for the whole camp.

"You know how to canoe?" I asked, feeling stupid as soon as the words were out of my mouth.

"Well, I was here last year, so I couldn't get away with going into the beginners' group, but it's not really my best thing. I'm always afraid I'll tip the boat over. I mean, if the canoe wasn't tippy why would we have to wear life jackets?"

"Listen up!" The murmuring of thirty girls quieted abruptly. "I'm going to review some basic stuff. Once I see that you know what you're doing, we'll practice getting in and out of the canoes. At the end of today's class I'll check you all on basic skills, and tomorrow maybe we can have some fun.

"You girls in the 'experienced' group, find a partner."

I looked at Nancy, but she'd already been claimed by a girl I didn't know. So had everybody else. Except me. And Jane.

Chapter Eighteen

Dear Sally,

You won't believe what happened in our first canoeing class. We had to partner up, and the only girls who couldn't find a partner were—guess who? Jane and me!

There was nothing to do about it. I couldn't exactly say I didn't want to be her partner, and she didn't like it any better than I did.

We split into two groups and were given paddles. The beginners were shown a few basic strokes—drawn on a blackboard, can you believe it? Then they were told to kneel on the edge of the dock and practice them.

My group got into canoes, two at a time, and paddled over to the swimming float and back. Jane insisted on the stern position, even though I've done lots more canoeing than she has. I just kept my head down and said nothing. I now know why people want to paddle in the back of the canoe.

They can talk their heads off and the bow paddler has to listen. Anyway, that's what Jane did. She talked about school (the most popular girl), the stable where she rides (best in the state), and her friends (the coolest ever). It's a good thing she couldn't see the look on my face!

To be honest, she paddles pretty well. Her forward stroke is strong and even, which helps a lot with keeping the canoe going straight. According to Jane, everything I did was wrong, and did she let me know it! I kept my mouth shut. Too bad I couldn't shut my ears.

We changed positions and paddled out to the raft again. Jane didn't like it this time.

After we put the canoes away (they're HEAVY), Gloria talked about safety. She handed out some sheets of rules to be tested on tomorrow.

Maybe I'll get to them, maybe I won't. I'd rather hang out with Cricket.

Please write.

Charley

Chapter Nineteen

I HAD TO GET AWAY from Jane. First swimming, now canoeing? I wasn't going to let her ruin my favorite camp activity. Easy to say, but how to make it happen?

I stomped through the woods on the way to see Cricket, skipping arts and crafts again. As I rounded the corner on my way to his paddock, I saw someone sitting with her back against a boulder, reading. It stopped me in my tracks. In my whole week at camp so far, I hadn't seen anyone with a book.

It was Birdie Johnson from New York City. Maybe we should form a Readers' Alliance Against Jane.

I walked over to where she was sitting, not sure whether to interrupt her. She looked up and smiled. "Hi, Charley," she said. "Pull up a rock and sit down."

"What are you reading?" I asked, feeling stupid and shy. I sat down next to her and waited for her to say something. I was thinking to get up and leave when she looked at me and put a finger in the book to hold her place.

"Sorry," she said. "I just had to finish that bit." She held up the book so I could read the title. "He's complicated. If I don't come to a good stopping place, I can't pick up where I left off."

The book was *The Souls of Black Folk*, by W.E.B. Dubois, a writer I'd never heard of.

"Does he write about horses?" I asked.

Birdie burst out laughing. "No," she said. "He wrote about freedom. He was an early civil rights leader who helped start the NAACP."

She looked at me curiously. "You've heard of that, right?"

I nodded, although "heard of it" was about all I could say. Current affairs are not my strong point.

"My father's writing a book about him, and that's why we're in New York." Birdie looked down at the book in her hand and made a face. "I thought I'd see what all the fuss was about, but he's pretty hard to read."

Silence fell on us. I couldn't think of anything else to say, and she probably wanted to get back to her book.

"Well, I better get going. If you ever want to borrow a book, I have about ten in my trunk."

"Really? I'd like that a lot!" Birdie tapped the book

in her hand. "I could use a break. Are you in my canoeing section? I'm looking for a paddling partner."

"That'd be great!" I said. "I love canoeing."

"I don't know about you," Birdie added, "but there are some people I'd rather not have in my canoe."

Massive understatement. "Same here. I don't really know anybody yet, so I get paired with people nobody else wants." Also a massive understatement, but I didn't want to whine about Jane. "Are we ever allowed to just paddle around with friends?"

"Yeah. You have to pass the first test. It's real simple. Just the basic strokes."

Birdie looked back down at her book. She wanted to read, not talk.

I got up to go. It was okay. I really needed to visit Cricket.

Chapter Twenty

I WOKE UP BEFORE REVEILLE with an aching knot in my stomach. Sally hadn't answered any of my letters, even though I checked my mailbox a million times a day.

No mail would come today. A mail-free day was both bad and good. Bad, because there would be no chance of a letter from Sally. Good, because I wouldn't get any mail from my parents either.

I'd told them to write together or not at all, but they'd each sent a letter anyway. Dad's was from his new apartment in Great Barrington. Mom's, of course, was from home. I stashed them at the bottom of my trunk and pretended they'd never arrived. Even thinking about them made my eyes tear up.

It was Sunday, the most boring day of the week at camp. No activities at all, just arts and crafts and other pointless time wasters. You could go for an after-lunch hike with your counselor if you wanted, but who wants to waste a walk in the woods on a counselor?

I felt a tiny twinge of guilt. I really like Carol,

but still. . . .

Along with the guilt came a good idea. I slid out of the bunk as quietly as I could, put jeans, sneakers and a sweatshirt on over my pj's, and snuck out onto the porch. I tried to step around the squeaky board in front of the door—they must have put it there on purpose—but it let out a shrill squeal. Jane snorted and rolled over in her bunk.

The sun was just rising, and mist still covered the lake. It looked spooky and smelled damp and musty. Or maybe the smell was from pine needles rotting on the ground behind the cabin. I started walking to the noss, then turned and headed for the trees instead. I could always pee behind a bush. The main thing was to get away without being seen. Cricket wouldn't care if I never brushed my teeth.

His field was misty, too. I squeezed through the top two rails. In less than a second my feet were soaked and freezing. Next time I'd wear socks.

I headed for Cricket's special spot and stopped. It didn't look right. There was a black blob on the ground under the tree, with a big yellow stripe at the bottom. I pictured some huge banana-shaped slug sucking out Cricket's entrails as he slept.

The big blob had to be Cricket, right? Was he

sleeping? With his neck stretched out and his head flat on the ground he looked dead. And what was the huge banana thing doing?

As if it could hear my thoughts, the banana lifted its head, wagged its tail and lay back down again, cuddled up against Cricket's warm belly.

Only a dog.

It stood up, stretched, and walked over to sniff my hand. As soon as I tried to pat it, the dog stood on its hind legs, put its paws on my shoulders and tipped me over. Then it sat on my stomach and started licking my face. I pushed it away and it sniffed my pockets, looking for food.

A big black nose nudged the dog out of the way and took over the sniffing.

I couldn't help laughing. Cricket put his nose close to mine, and we exchanged breath in a horse hello. Then he started eating the dew-drenched grass.

I squatted behind the tree, and Cricket politely looked the other way. Then I went to work on his back with the currycomb, rubbing the ridged oval in tight circles to loosen the dried mud. He turned his head around to look at me, and I gave his forehead a good scratch.

Next to eating, Cricket's favorite thing seems to be

getting down and dirty. I like cleaning him up. It always feels good when he's clean and shiny again.

Something bumped into my hip. I whipped around, and the dog backed up, put its forelegs on the grass and bowed, tail waving madly. It grabbed the currycomb and skipped backwards, staying just out of reach, then turned and ran away.

"Hey, get back here, you mangy yellow mutt!"

Time was flying, and I wanted to be back in the cabin before bugle call. The dog walked over, head down, currycomb still in its mouth. When I reached for it, the dog turned tail and raced off.

"Come on, chase me," it said, as clear as if speaking English. "Just a little chase? Then I'll give it back. I promise."

"Sheesh!" I needed to leave, but I needed the curry-comb more. I made one last grab, but the dog was having too much fun. Why stop a perfectly good game?

The first notes of reveille blasted over the loud-speaker. I turned around and ran.

Chapter Twenty-One

I DETOURED TO THE NOSS on the way back to the cabin. I had to catch my breath and take off the jeans and sweatshirt. I did some deep breathing and hid the rolled-up clothes behind the last toilet in the row. I'd grab them after breakfast and no one would be any wiser.

I was running out the door when I smacked face to face into you-know-who.

"Where've *you* been?" asked Jane, blocking the doorway.

I gave what I hoped was a convincing yawn and tried to edge past her.

"I woke up when you left this morning and couldn't get back to sleep. It was easy to follow your steps in the wet grass, but when you got to the woods I lost you."

"What business is it of yours? There's no law I ever heard about that says I can't go for a walk before breakfast."

"Just curious," Jane said. "Did you see the big dog

following you back here? You never know with stray dogs. It might have rabies or scabies or something. You don't want to bring it back to the cabin. I'm sure there are laws about *that*."

"So call the cops, why don't you?" I pushed past her and headed back to change.

"Don't forget your clothes!"

She always has to get in the last word, I thought. I won't give her the satisfaction.

Yellow Dog—it was a girl, I found out—was waiting for me. She sauntered out from under the porch stairs and sat. I leaned down and whispered in her floppy yellow ear.

"If you want to do me a real favor, keep that girl away from me. You can track her by the nasty smell she leaves behind."

Chapter Twenty-Two

IT WAS STORY NIGHT, A Secret Lake tradition. Anyone who wants to can sign up to tell a story. There's only one rule: it has to be scary.

Tonight Sarah Potetti, a senior from Cabin Eleven, had the floor. We sat around the campfire, stuffed with barbecued chicken and potato salad, and waited.

"It was a dark and stormy night. . . ."

The opening line was not a big hit. She got a chorus of boos and raspberries and had to start over.

"Alright, already! No stormy night! Give me a minute to think. How about this? 'Once upon a time. . . .'"

More boos and catcalls. Somebody threw a wadded-up napkin.

"Okay," she said. "Have you ever heard"—she lowered her voice—"about . . . the Creature . . . from the . . . Black . . . Lagoon?"

Nobody said a word.

I could have said plenty. My dad took Jeremy and

me to see the movie when I was ten. Mom was pretty mad, but what could she do? We couldn't *un*see it, could we? Anyway, the nightmares only lasted about a week, so no big deal.

I knew I wouldn't be scared, but it would be interesting to see how Sarah told the story. She might put in a few neat twists, and I had no place else to be.

"It started in the Amazon jungle, a strange misty world with man-eating fish, poison darts, and tribes so isolated they had never seen white men. A land of head hunters and strangler vines hanging from trees whose tops were hidden in the clouds."

Sarah paused while we all settled in for a long creepy listen.

"A group of geologists was sent to Brazil to sample unique rock formations found in the rain forest, but so far they hadn't seen any rocks at all. Just rotted leaves and fallen branches, covering the forest floor to an unknowable depth.

"All day a grayish light struggled to penetrate the leaf canopy high above, and the air was so thick you could drink it. Biting insects swarmed all night, driving the scientists to distraction. They heard no other living creature, not even a bird, though they knew the forest teemed with life.

"And, everywhere, the feeling of being watched.

"The eyes of the jungle never left them. If the native guides shot a peccary or a deer and roasted it for supper, yellow predator eyes in the shadows followed their every move. Leaves quivered and shadows moved where there was no wind, but they never saw another living thing."

I felt a chill on my neck. This was one scary story. I had to make up the pictures in my own head, and they made the movie look like *Fantasia*.

Sarah continued, her voice getting lower and huskier as she talked. "Every week or so they found a village and stocked up on supplies. Salt and bread, flour and lard. They quizzed the villagers about the native Indians, about the shadows and the eyes, but the local people looked away and didn't answer.

"One day it all changed. A cliff, covered with vines and nearly invisible, pushed out of the jungle in front of them. It lay on its side, slanting upwards like a huge upturned boat, with one big crack opening it up to the scientists' greedy eyes.

"The rock face, where it had broken, was covered with fossils. Skeleton fish, trilobites, and horseshoe crabs crowded one another, all turned to stone in the rock. In the middle was something not to be believed:

an arm, only bones, attached to a very human-looking hand."

Someone screamed.

"Marshmallows, anyone? It's time for s'mores!" Counselors moved to the fire with Hershey bars, graham crackers, and all the marshmallows anyone could want.

Birdie and I collected the makings. She waved a small white cylinder in the air. "You know about these, right?" she asked. I didn't, but I knew she was about to tell me. "Sugar," she said. "Pure sugar. They whip it up and it turns into this. I wonder why it tastes so good."

There was a crowd toasting marshmallows, so we took ours back to my spot and sat down.

"What do you think about the story?" I asked. "Do you think it's scary?"

"I don't see it," she said. "No way can fossilized human bones show up in the same layer as trilobites. There's this whole thing about it at the Museum of Natural History in Washington, D.C. My dad took me. We were there for some kind of conference, and he had a free afternoon. Mom went shopping or something."

Trust Birdie to turn a scary story into a history report.

"Come on. It's just a pretend. Put your brilliant mind to work on this, then. Who screamed?"

"I thought it was Jane," Birdie said. "Well, it would be, wouldn't it? Either she was really scared, in which case she's too stupid to live, or she just wanted attention. I vote for attention. What do you think?"

"I think there's room at the fire. Let's go burn some sugar."

I WAS TRYING TO MAKE marshmallow toffee but only made a mess. I licked the fractured candy off my fingers.

Sarah went back to her place and we all sat down.

"Where was I?" Sarah asked. "Oh, yeah. The wall. The scientists swarmed over the split in the rock and examined it as well as they could with the instruments at hand. It didn't match any known rocks in that whole sector of Brazil, and the fossils left them frankly baffled.

"Then the cook and his assistant went to the river and didn't come back. When supper failed to appear the scientists were annoyed, then concerned, then frankly worried. They went to the river to look.

"Blood on the bank, signs of a struggle, the scuffed and bloody print of a crooked webbed foot. Within hours the camp had been dismantled. What couldn't be carried was abandoned. At first light the whole expedition, hunters, porters, servants and all, raced back to civilization. They didn't make it. Only one geologist, traumatized past speech, arrived in Menaus, and from there was flown home to California.

"More expeditions went to the jungle. More bloody footprints on the riverbank. Research on the link between creatures of the water and dwellers on the land became frenzied, and a theory was put forward about a hybrid humanoid, sensitive to the smell of blood, that haunted the edges of the world's greatest river searching for an easy meal.

"Water Man, he was called—although the name didn't carry with it any of the dread felt by the few who had seen his tracks and the ruin he left behind. Only the lone escaped scientist made the connection between the footprint on the bank and the hand in the rock, and he wasn't talking.

"Years passed. Other strange incidents were reported, always on the banks of rivers, always involving blood. Soon every continent had its own story of a water creature that walked on dry land and killed at will."

The counselors were in a huddle, talking softly.

Mrs. Behrens walked over to the fire.

"That's enough, girls. Time for hot chocolate and a song." Groans from the campers.

"No, no, story's over for tonight. We don't want any Water Men visiting your dreams."

It figured. Just when the story was getting interesting we had to go to bed.

Chapter Twenty-Three

I HATE LEARNING TO POST! I really do. Why can't I ride like I do in my dreams, bareback, sliding back and forth, rocking to the horse's movement like they do in the movies? Nobody posts in the Wild West.

Actually, I thought, nobody trots much in the Wild West, either. Everything seems to happen at the gallop.

Oh, well, I told myself. Don't worry about it. You've got twelve whole hours before you have to face Firefly's trot again. I yawned widely enough to dislocate my jaw, turned onto my side and fell into sleep.

It was a chaotic night, full of dreams and fragments of dreams. I couldn't really sleep but couldn't seem to wake up, either. When reveille finally blared through the loudspeakers, I was exhausted.

Yesterday's unhappy lesson spread itself out for me, exactly as it had happened. I couldn't post to the trot, and Lois was sick and tired of hearing me gripe about it.

"You don't like posting?" she said. "Fine. You don't

have to post. Ask Firefly for a trot and just sit there."

That sounded more like it! I felt happy for about half a second, then looked for the catch.

"Well, go ahead," Lois said. "Ask him to trot."

Here goes nothing, I thought. "Firefly, trot!"

I felt like a carrot in a Waring blender, bouncing around all over the place. By the time I managed to say whoa, I had lost both stirrups and was hanging on to the saddle for dear life.

"Ready to try it my way?" Lois asked.

What could I say?

"The trot is a very up-and-down gait. Rising and sitting to the rhythm of the trot—posting—is a way to smooth the gait out. Like magic, the bouncing is gone."

I got the message. Posting was my friend. That didn't mean I could do it. No matter what I tried, I couldn't rise. I flopped back into the saddle every time.

Firefly got sick of having his mouth pulled and started pinning his ears whenever I asked him to trot. Hard as I worked to get it right, I was hurting him.

When the lesson was finally over, I offered him half an apple to say sorry. He turned his head away and walked into his stall.

Chapter Twenty-Four

IT WAS TIME FOR MY lesson, but I wanted to pull the covers over my head, put my fingers in my ears, and go back to sleep. I'd never get away with it. Lois would come and roust me out.

I sighed and pulled on my jods. They'd stretched out enough at the waist to be comfortable, and even the boots felt like they belonged to me. I grabbed my favorite sweatshirt, the one Birdie gave me that says "I'd rather be reading," and dragged it down over my head. Who cared how my hair looked? It would be stuffed underneath that stupid helmet.

Firefly was standing in the aisle. He checked to see if I had more apples, then pretended I wasn't there. I went through the drill: curry, brush, de-twig his mane, pretend to comb out his tail. I steeled myself to pick out his hooves, but he lifted them for me without complaint.

I put the saddle pad on and pulled it down like I'd been taught. Then I carried his saddle to the aisle so

Lois could put it on Firefly. She lifted it on to his back and settled it gently into place. As she buckled up the girth, she started to talk.

"Today we're going to try something different. You're having trouble with posting because your legs slide forward when you rise in the stirrups. You don't feel—in your body—where your legs need to be.

"You're not alone. Most people don't really 'feel' where their body parts are at any given time. They just have a vague idea. So I'm going to help you put your legs where they belong. By the end of today's lesson, you'll be able to feel it. Even better, you'll have a way to test the feeling. I'm sure Firefly will be very relieved."

I had no idea what she was talking about. Of course I know where my legs are. They're *my* legs!

"Mount up and get settled. I'll meet you in the arena."

I was just about to put my foot in the stirrup when a voice in my head whispered *Check it again. He's a master at blowing out.* Sure enough, the girth was still loose. I tightened it another two holes and mounted at the block. We walked through the barn door and into the arena.

Lois came out carrying his halter and lead rope.

"You're going to think this is crazy, but trust me. It

works. Put the reins down on his neck. You won't need them. Now stand up in the stirrups. Stand right up, as tall as you can."

I did my best, but every time I got even a little bit out of the saddle, I fell backwards. It was embarrassing. How hard could it be to stand in the stirrups?

I tried it another way, gripping the saddle with my calves and using his mane to pull myself up. No good. I was amazed Firefly stood so quietly while I flopped around with his mane in my fists.

"Why do you think you can't stand up?" Lois asked.

I shook my head and mumbled. She tied the reins in a knot and put the halter on over Firefly's bridle. "Look at me. I'm standing. Where are my legs?"

"On the ground," I said. Stupid question. Where else would they be?

"My feet are on the ground. Where are my legs?"

I really hate trick questions. I looked. Her legs were right over her feet, straight up to her hips. The rest of her was right over her hips.

"You are standing straight," I said grumpily. "Your legs are over your feet. So what?"

"How about if my legs were behind my feet?" She leaned back as much as she could without falling over. To keep her balance, she'd have to move back over her feet.

"Oh," I said. "I get it."

"It's all about position," Lois said. "You need to sit in such balance that if the horse were whipped out from under you, you'd be standing on your feet."

I frankly couldn't imagine sitting on a horse that way, but I had to give it a try.

I pressed my knees against the saddle for leverage, leaned forward, and grabbed a handful of mane to pull myself up a few inches.

My legs couldn't fly backward because my knees were pinned.

It took forever but, by increments, reaching higher and higher up his mane, I made it to a sort of standing crouch. Then I pushed my feet down into the stirrups and stood up, with my arms out wide for balance. It felt like I'd scaled a pyramid!

Lois made me do the whole thing about a million times, but finally I had it. Then she changed the game, and I almost went right back to the beginning.

"Keep your knees loose," she said. "It's a little like riding a bike or a surfboard. If you lock your knees, your balance disappears. I'm going to lead Firefly around the ring. See if you can stay on your feet."

I was sure I'd tumble straight to the ground, but it

didn't go that way. Once I had my balance, I kept it.

"If you're ever unsure about where your legs are," Lois smiled, "just stand up in the stirrups. It automatically puts you where you need to be. Tomorrow we'll try it at the trot. You'll be amazed."

I'll just bet I will, I thought.

Lois had been right about one thing, though.

Firefly did look relieved.

Chapter Twenty-Five

I COULDN'T STOP HANGING OVER the fence. Cricket looked pretty healthy now, but I knew different. I couldn't get the pictures of the last twelve hours out of my head.

It started when Yellow Dog ambushed me on the way to the noss. I don't know much about dogs, so when she grabbed my towel in her teeth and pulled, I thought she wanted to play tug of war. Every time I pulled back, she dropped her end and woofed at me. It was annoying, because I really, really had to pee. What did she want?

I dropped the towel, did what I had to do, and came out with dripping hands. She still had one end of the towel in her mouth. I made a grab for it, but she turned and ran into the woods. She kept checking to see if I was following, which of course I was. I wanted my towel back.

We ran straight to Cricket's paddock. I couldn't see him, but Yellow Dog woofed some more—it wasn't a real bark, more like a grunt—and led me through the fence and over a small rise to where he was lying on the grass.

He didn't look good. In fact he looked terrible. I knew that for an actual fact, but I didn't know how I knew it. Horses' faces aren't made to show emotion but, once you know the horse, you can tell when something's wrong.

Cricket was lying on his side, but he wasn't resting. His head was off the ground and his nose almost touched his belly. His lips were pulled tight against his teeth and pointed down at the corners. His eyes were open, but he wasn't looking at anything.

I stood in front of him, wondering what to do. Was he hurt? Was he sick? Was he just in a bad mood? Do horses have bad moods?

I ran to the barn. Lois was in the arena teaching a lesson.

"The black horse is sick!" I yelled. "Something's wrong."

Lois came over to the fence.

"What's going on? What does he look like?" I explained as well as I could. It wasn't much because I didn't know anything. "We'd better call the vet." She walked back into the lesson. "Everybody turn your horses' heads to the rail and stay put. I'll be right back."

She walked quickly to the office and started dialing. I heard her talking but couldn't make out the words.

She came back out to the ring. "Charley, the vet is on his way. Go back and wait with your horse until the vet arrives. I'll be there in a minute." She waved at one of the seniors who'd been sitting in the sun cleaning tack.

"Angie, please take the lesson. Over the cavaletti one at a time, slow trot. When everyone has gone once, pick up the pace to a working trot." She turned to the class. "The point here, ladies, is *straight.* I'll be back as soon as I can, and we'll set up a few jumps."

I sprinted back to Cricket. She'd called him *my* horse!

LOIS GOT THERE RIGHT AFTER me, so she must have run, too. She looked him over and put her ear to his belly. Then she picked up his halter and buckled it on.

"Come on, beauty, up you get." She pulled gently on the lead rope, talking all the time, and in a minute he was on his feet.

He didn't look happy.

"I think it might be colic," she said. "The best thing

to do is keep him moving." She handed me the lead. "Walk him around in a big circle and don't let him lie down. If he drops some manure it's a good thing. We can show it to the vet when he gets here."

Lois went back to the barn, leaving me in charge.

Cricket and I must have walked a hundred miles before a shiny red truck pulled up to the gate and a man got out. He looked like a farmer in his Levi's and plaid flannel shirt, but I hoped he was the vet at last. He pulled a big leather satchel off the passenger seat, and I breathed a sigh of relief. My throat was sore from singing "Speed Bonnie Boat" over and over again. It was the only song I could think of, and I only knew one verse.

"I'm Dr. Sayers," he said, "and this must be Promise. What seems to be the problem?"

While I told him the story he pulled out a stethoscope and listened to the horse's belly. Then he slid a thermometer under Cricket's tail and counted off seconds on a big silvery watch. He took Cricket's—or should I say *Promise's*—pulse and, I think, counted his breaths.

"Any manure?"

I shook my head. My chest was getting tighter and tighter, and I could feel my face twisting into its I'm-going-to-cry-any-second shape. I swallowed hard and tried to listen to what the vet was saying.

"There are no bowel sounds, and his pulse and respiration are elevated."

I had no idea what that meant, but it didn't sound good. Yellow Dog came over and stuck her head under my hand, offering comfort. It helped, but not enough.

"Is he going to be okay?"

"Hmm? Okay? Oh, yes. I was worried about Potomac. There's been some around here, but he has no fever, so that's good. He's got a bit of colic and I'll medicate him for it. Keep him on his feet and walking. That's the best thing."

The vet rooted around in his bag and brought out an enormous syringe and a large tube of what looked like toothpaste. He connected the tube to the syringe and squeezed in about two inches worth of white goop.

He handed me the lead rope, pushed the end of the syringe into the side of Cricket's mouth, and squirted the stuff in. Crick made horrible faces but he swallowed it.

"Banamine. It will relax him and stop the spasms. Colic really hurts, and in bad cases the pain can put a horse into shock and kill him." My face must have looked funny, because he hurried to say the rest. "Keep him walking until he makes some manure. He can drink a little, but not much. He probably won't want to anyway. If he tries to lie down, make him walk."

Lois finally came back. She and the vet moved away from me and talked too quietly for me to hear. My chest tightened even more, and I started to cough.

Dr. Sayers said walk so we walked, me on one side and Yellow Dog on the other. I was wearing my watch, and I timed it. Walk for ten minutes, rest for two. Walk ten minutes more. I'd calmed down a little and remembered more songs.

When I started the Toreador Song from *Carmen*, Cricket stopped and stared at me. Maybe he was an opera fan like my dad. I clucked at him, and we walked some more.

I heard the bugle call for swimming, and then the one for lunch. I was getting really, really hungry. Lois stopped by to see how we were doing.

"Any manure?"

"No. Is that bad?"

"It's early days yet," Lois said. "I'll be happy when he drops some, though. It'll mean his gut has decided to work again. You look a little white around the mouth. Want me to take over for a bit?"

I didn't, but I did. I was starving and needed the

bathroom. I handed over the lead rope, told Cricket I'd be right back, and rushed towards the cabins. I looked around for Yellow Dog, but she had disappeared.

"Hey, Charley!"

Birdie ran down the path, waving something in the air that looked like a sandwich. I was hungry enough to eat anything, even the dreaded ham salad. I peeled off the wax paper. Whew! It was turkey and lettuce.

The sandwich was kind of dry, and I coughed a little trying to get it down. Birdie held out a carton of chocolate milk. It tasted like heaven. We walked to the noss together, and I told her about the colic and how Cricket's gut had stopped working. I had to pinch my leg hard to keep from crying. Birdie didn't say anything. She just walked with me back to the fence.

I took the lead rope and introduced Birdie to Cricket. He seemed a little brighter, but when I looked a question at Lois, she shook her head. No manure yet.

Lois left to take some intermediates out on a trail ride. Birdie went to archery. Yellow Dog came back, and I gave her the crust from my sandwich. She took her position on Cricket's off side and walked with us.

We walked. And walked. And walked. For one tiny second it occurred to me: my whole world now revolved around horse poop.

The bugle called again to signal the next activity. I was too tired to think what it was. Cricket stopped walking. Then, as casually as could be, as if we hadn't been waiting for it all day, he dropped some manure and leaned down to crop up a mouthful of grass.

Chapter Twenty-Six

BREAKFAST WAS EGGS, SUNNY SIDE up—yuck! I grabbed a piece of toast and headed for the barn. The sooner the lesson was over, the sooner I could hang out with Cricket.

Firefly snatched the toast right out of my hand and let me pull burrs out of his mane while he chewed. Is he starting to like me? Probably he just likes toast.

I pawed through the grooming box for a big comb. What I really needed was cream rinse, but guess what? No cream rinse in the barn. Nancy says Brylcreem works even better. I'll ask around. In the meantime, it was fingers, one burr at a time. I tried to comb the burr-less bits, but it was a losing battle.

I picked up the currycomb and went to work. As I leaned into him big swirls of dirt came to the surface of his back. What does he do out there to get so dirty?

I was brushing away the last of the grime when Lois walked in. She looked Firefly over extra carefully, not saying a word. Then she blew on his back and ruffled up his coat.

What did she see? Was it a lousy job? Couldn't I get anything right?

"Good work, Charley. You catch on really fast. He won't get saddle sores today, that's for sure. If you pick out his feet, I'll get his tack. We have a lot to do today and not a lot of time."

So now I had three things to worry about. I had to pick up Firefly's feet, gouge out any dirt with a hoof pick, and wonder what Lois had planned for the lesson.

I ran a hand down the back of each leg, and when he politely lifted the foot I checked carefully for stones. All clear. No digging required. I gave him a pat.

Lois tacked him up in no time, almost before I'd finished with the hoof pick. I brought his bridle over, put on my helmet, and waited. Lois picked up his reins and started to walk.

She led the way to the big sliding door at the front of the barn. Something was wrong. We always go to the arena, and Lois always makes me lead Firefly.

I started to worry for real.

Lois handed me the reins. "Mount up and wait for me here. I'll be right back."

I checked Firefly's girth and tightened it one hole at a time.

"Good job," Lois said, looking back. "Always wise to check the girth. Especially his."

Firefly shuffled his feet, and I knew he was thinking about playing games, but I growled at him and he stood still. I don't know who was more shocked, him or me. Or maybe Lois.

I mounted without any drama and looked at my hands on the reins. They were shaking. I shrugged inside. I had to ride him, but nobody said I had to be a hero.

Lois went back inside the barn. Firefly and I looked at the empty space where she'd been standing.

What were we supposed to do? Was this a test?

Firefly shuffled his feet some more. He'd stood still long enough. Okay, what now? I did the only thing I could think of. "Firefly," I said. "Walk up."

Lois stayed in the barn for a long, long time. We'd already done diagonals, circles (in both directions), and were working on figure eights.

"Whoa," I said, and Firefly stood still. I patted his neck and scratched a little under his mane. Here we were, all alone and still on track. We deserved a medal.

"What are you doing out here all on your lonesome? Where's your babysitter?"

I didn't need to look around to know who was talking.

"I'm speaking to you," Jane said, with a nasty edge to her voice. "Cat got your tongue?"

I started another figure eight. It was pretty wobbly, but definitely better than standing still. Firefly was pretending to be the perfect dressage horse. Jane sulked and looked angry. As usual. I had to giggle. The whole thing was too stupid to take seriously.

"I didn't know you were allowed off the lead rein. Maybe some—"

"We're going on a trail ride," Lois said.

When I turned around, Jane was gone. Lois was leading a tall bay mare named Angel. Nancy said she was called that because she could be a real devil.

"A trail ride?" I asked. "Isn't that a little advanced for me?"

"We need to put a little fun into the lessons. Otherwise, why would you bother to learn?"

Good question. Why indeed?

Lois checked Angel's girth, put her foot in the stirrup, and landed on the saddle as softly as a bird alights on a branch. I was dripping with envy. No matter how many lessons I struggled through, I'd never mount a horse like Lois did.

"It just takes practice," she said, reading my mind. "You'll get the knack. Being nearly six feet tall helps, too. Have you ever noticed how many riders are tall?"

That leaves me out. Maybe I'll learn to levitate.

Lois pointed to the halter and lead rope she'd tied around her waist.

"If you want, we can use Firefly's halter and I can hold on to the lead rope, but honestly, Charley, I don't think you need it. Your figure eights were looking pretty good, and he did everything you asked. You won't have any trouble out on the trail."

I decided to believe the compliment. I could go for a little fun, and Firefly could probably use some, too.

"Trail riding is very different from working in the arena," Lois said. "For one thing, the horses enjoy it more. They love being outside just bopping along. You'll feel a difference in Firefly as soon as we're away from the barn."

She was right. Firefly's walk became quicker and more powerful. His ears were pricked, and he looked around, sniffing the air. Maybe he was too quick. Maybe he'd decide to run away. He probably hated lessons, and if he got rid of me maybe he'd never have to teach a beginner again. . . .

"Charley!" Lois' voice was sharp. "You're hunched over like you have a stomachache. Sit up and look between Firefly's ears to where you want to go."

I tried. I really tried, but I didn't like this trail ride stuff one bit.

"Why are we doing this?" I whined. "We were fine in the ring." The big outdoors was looking way too big, and my stomach had started to hurt for real.

"Sit up straight and take long deep breaths. Let the air out slowly."

I took as deep a breath as I could, but my lungs were shut.

"Do you know any good poems?" Lois asked. "There's nothing like a good poem to make a ride go more smoothly."

"Poems?" Was she crazy? Firefly was about to bolt and she wanted to know about *poetry*?

"I didn't do much poetry in school," Lois said. "I love to listen to it. What's your favorite poem?"

I mumbled something under my breath. It was a good thing she didn't hear it.

She cleared her throat. It was code for "get with the program."

"Jabberwocky," I said quickly. "I like that one a lot."

"Say it for me. I'll bet Firefly likes poetry too."

"'Twas brillig, and the slithy toves,
Did gyre and gimble in the wabe. . . .'"

I got so wrapped up in all the funny made-up words, I forgot about Firefly. He was still powering along, but it's not like he was galloping away or anything.

When I was done with the poem, Lois halted Angel and Firefly stopped next to her. We both blew out a big breath.

"Have a look at your hands," Lois said. "Are the reins tight? Are you pulling on his mouth?"

My hands looked fine. Relaxed, even. They rested on the front of the saddle, minding their own business.

"When you got tense back there, when it felt like Firefly was going too fast, you did what any untrained rider would do. You pulled on the reins to slow him down.

"Didn't work, did it?"

I shook my head, remembering the panicky feeling when Firefly didn't listen.

"Pulling on a horse's mouth always seems like a good idea, and it almost never works. What happens is just the opposite. When you pull on him, he pulls back. So you pull harder. The next thing you know, the horse feels like he's running away with you. What he's running away from is your hard hands."

"So how do you get him to slow down?" I asked.

The subject was making me angry. I'd done the best I could and what did I get? A lecture on how I did it wrong.

"You relax. Sounds simple, doesn't it? It's not. How do you relax when you're scared, and the situation seems to be getting out of control? Any ideas?"

I shook my head again.

"You change the subject. Think about something else. Some people sing. You recited poetry. You got lost in the poem and forgot to think about Firefly. And as soon as you relaxed, even a tiny bit, he relaxed a little, too. So did your hands. Without the pull on his mouth, Firefly could stop pulling back.

"And here's something else. When you're tense, you often hold your breath. It's natural. Everybody does it. Holding your breath makes the horse even tenser, which makes you tenser still. It's a vicious circle. Fortunately for both of you, there's an easy solution. When you're singing, or talking, or reciting poetry, you can't hold your breath."

Somewhere along the line we'd started walking again and I hadn't even noticed! Firefly's walk was still kind of fast, but his head was down and his ears looked floppy. His back was swinging under me, and it felt good. I felt good, too.

"We're having this little introduction to trail riding because I want you in with the beginners by the end of the week. You've come a long way in an amazingly short time, and you're ready to join the class."

I'd be happy to stay away from any class that had Jane in it. If I spent the whole summer going around in circles in the arena, it would be okay with me.

Lois, it seemed, did not agree.

"The class is going on a trail ride, and I want you and Firefly to be part of it. It'll only be a short walk through the woods and across a field. I know the two of you will do just fine."

That makes one of us, I thought. I really don't want to do this.

"Tomorrow we'll hack out again, following the same route the class will follow. Your confidence will be up for this. I promise."

We walked along, with me practicing the things I'd learned in the ring: shoulders back, head up, breathing. I was starting to feel pretty good, confident even. I can do this, I thought. I really can.

There was a screech of brakes, a crash, and the sound of a million bottles breaking at once. Firefly leaped sideways. I lost my balance, and Yellow Dog ran across the trail with her tail between her legs.

I ended up with my arms around Firefly's neck, holding on for dear life. I slid to the ground and stood next to him, stroking his neck and whispering Jabberwocky. Carrots would have been better, but there are no pockets in my jods.

Firefly calmed down a lot faster than I did.

I looked around for Lois. She was way down the track turning Angel in small circles and swearing. At least that's what it looked like. I guess Angel really does have a devil in her head. I leaned my head against Firefly's neck, grateful that whatever else was wrong with him, he didn't have any devils.

Chapter Twenty-Seven

Dear Sally,

Just when I think I'm getting the hang of this riding thing, Lois ups the ante. She's decided I need experience riding outside the ring, and that means trail rides. I didn't have time to worry about it. We went out right then and there.

I was pretty nervous, but Firefly has been on so many rides he could do them in his sleep. We were doing okay, and I was starting to relax and have a good time, when the crash came.

It sounded like the end of the world and smelled like Coca-Cola. Lois' horse, Angel, panicked and tried to run away. Firefly just jumped a little, and I didn't fall off.

Here's what happened: A guy was delivering bottles of soda for the machine outside the dining hall. Yellow Dog—have I told you about her? She hangs out with Cricket all the time—ran in front of the truck, and the driver had to swerve. He lost control and crashed into a stone wall. Every bottle in the truck was smashed to smithereens. The road was covered with green glass and swimming in Coca-Cola.

Too bad about wasting all that pop.

Watching Lois get Angel under control was almost as cool as the crash. She pulled Angel round and round in really tight circles until she calmed down and stopped fighting. It took a few tries, but finally the mare stood still. You should have heard Lois! I'm surprised grownups even know those words!

It's good to know instructors have bad horse days, too, but my troubles are just beginning. Next week is my first group lesson. I'm not sure who will be there, but dollars to donuts Jane will be in the group.

I'm a nice person, kind and considerate. What did I do to deserve Jane Blake?

I'll write and tell you all about it—if I survive.

Do you like trail rides?

Love,
Charley

P.S. The driver, who's pretty cute, wasn't badly hurt. Neither was Yellow Dog.

Chapter Twenty-Eight

THE BIG DAY: FIREFLY AND I were joining the beginners' class for the first time. I was nervous about it but not paralyzed. Not yet, anyway. Just in case I was—paralyzed, that is—Lois sent Nancy to help me get ready.

We went through all the warm-up exercises I did every day with Lois, but today they felt different. I was far away, watching Firefly circle the ring—while the girl on his back swung her arms and legs, and then took her feet out of the stirrups and put them back in without kicking the horse in the ribs.

It wasn't me on Firefly's back. I was the Watcher.

I wasn't afraid, exactly. I just wasn't there.

After a few minutes Nancy noticed something was wrong and called me into the middle of the ring. I watched myself steer Firefly to the letter X, say whoa, and stop. I didn't know how to get back into my own skin and, believe me, that was scary!

"Keep Firefly walking," Nancy said. "I won't be

a second."

She came back with a bottle of Coke and a silly grin. "I think you need a caffeine jolt," she said. "Whatever you do, don't tell Carol."

I never drink Coke or any other soft drinks. Mom doesn't buy them, and I never developed a taste. But maybe drastic measures were called for. I took a couple of big swigs of icy cold fizz, choked, and landed back in my body where I belonged. I scrubbed my face with cold hands, sat straight in the saddle, and waited for Nancy to tell me what to do next.

She looked at her watch. "Not much time left. Let's go straight to the trot."

Gulp. Definitely not my favorite thing.

"Don't worry," Nancy said. "You won't have to do a lot of trotting in class today. Look for the letter B over there. Walk to B, turn right and trot all the way around the ring to A, come down to the walk, go up the center line to X and stop in front of me."

How was I going to remember all that? I studied the letters. Trot at B, all the way around the ring to A, then walk up the center line. It didn't look hard. I wondered what the catch was.

There wasn't one. Firefly didn't want to stop at X, but I think he was trying to be funny. When I said whoa again, he stopped.

Jane was the first one to come into the ring. She pretended I wasn't there, and I returned the compliment. I kept Firefly moving around the ring, and Jane did the same with Jack.

Then Evie brought Rocket to the mounting block, tightened his girth, and swung into the saddle. For a solid girl she's very light in her movements. Where I land on Firefly with a thump, she seems to weigh nothing. I comforted myself with the thought that she was taller than me so getting on was easier—but in my heart I know that with the mounting block height doesn't count.

Three girls I knew only by sight walked in with their horses and lined up next to the block. Birdie came next leading Mosby. She is tiny, and Mosby is definitely not, but they somehow seem made for each other.

I hadn't known I'd have friends in the class. If I made a fool of myself it wouldn't be so bad. Then Carol walked in carrying a clipboard and I went limp with relief.

Two instructors teach the beginner classes, Carol and Ingeborg. Inga is Norwegian and really strict. Nothing but total commitment and heroic effort is good enough for her, even from beginners. The advanced students follow her around like puppies, but the rest of us cringe whenever her name is mentioned.

I was SO glad Carol was our teacher.

"Okay, girls, let's get started."

All the chatter died away. Carol has a soft voice, and you have to concentrate to hear her.

"Line up on the rail, please, with at least two horses' lengths between you. Jane, you can lead. Then Evie, Charley, Sandy, Jennifer and Carolyn. Birdie, you and Mosby can take up the rear."

After a little shuffling around we were all set. I didn't know Sandy's horse, but Firefly didn't seem to care, so I didn't either.

"Pick up your reins, sit deep and prepare to walk." A few seconds silence, then, in a singing kind of voice, "Walk, please."

I squeezed with my legs and Firefly walked. I practically bumped into Rocket's rump, and then pulled on the reins to make Firefly walk slower. Instead, he stopped dead. A traffic jam piled up behind me.

I wanted to die.

"To slow your horse down, close your fingers on the reins. No need to pull. Let's try it again." Carol spoke to the whole class, but I felt like she was talking to me: the only camper in the whole world who didn't know how to ride.

This time I got it right, or maybe it was just that Firefly figured out what was wanted and did it.

I managed to get through most of the hour without anything awful happening. Jane made faces at me every chance she got, but what else was new? Even the trot around the ring to the back of the line was accomplished without a problem.

Nancy walked beside me on the outside of the ring. If I didn't understand an instruction, she translated into horse-free English.

I didn't fall off or cause anyone else to fall. Firefly followed my aids before I even gave them. He probably understood exactly what Carol was saying—better than I did, anyway.

When we were asked to trot a figure-eight one at a time using the whole arena, I panicked. There was something about diagonals I had to know, but I couldn't remember what. Carol told me to wait on the rail and watch.

"You can try it next time," she said.

Jane muttered something snide, too softly to hear.

The lesson was finally over, and we took our horses back to the barn. Firefly wasn't even damp under his saddle pad. I brushed him and gave him a big kiss. He pretended not to know me, so I took the carrot I had hidden in my waistband and handed it over. He'd been a good generous boy and deserved it.

CAROL CALLED ME OVER AS I was leaving.

"You did a great job for your first group lesson ever," she said. "I didn't realize you hadn't learned to rate your horse, but how could you without other horses to follow?"

I felt like an idiot. Lois made me practice slowing down and speeding up at the walk in my lessons. I just didn't understand that Carol was asking for the same thing, only with other horses in the ring. And I certainly knew better than to pull on Firefly's mouth.

"Tell me," Carol said. "What did you learn today?"

I had to think.

"Looking ahead. I didn't know how important it was to look ahead and see what the horse in front was doing in time to do it too."

That sounded pretty lame, but Carol understood what I meant. She nodded.

"You have to have eyes in front, in back and on both sides of your head. When riding in a group you have to know what everyone is doing all the time. Then you can stay in control of your horse. If you're out in the clouds somewhere, everything that happens is a surprise."

How was I going to learn to see in all directions at once? Especially without turning my head?

"It takes time and practice," Carol said, before I could ask. "Don't worry, you'll get there. In the meantime I'll have Nancy babysit you during the lessons. You did well today, and I'm sure you'll do even better tomorrow."

Nancy, Birdie and Evie were waiting outside, and the three girls I didn't know were hanging around too. Nancy introduced us, looking embarrassed. "I should have done this at the beginning. Sorry."

The bugle called for the next activity. For me it was arts and crafts, but not today. I was too happy. I ran right past the A&C pavilion, all the way to Cricket's field. He was at the fence waiting to hear all about the lesson. I couldn't wait to tell him.

Chapter Twenty-Nine

I WAS NOT ENJOYING THE trail ride. Okay, so I'd done it twice with Lois. Okay, so Firefly had more time on the trails than any horse God ever made. Okay, so everyone else on the ride had experience to burn. I was still scared to death. My heart was beating so hard it wanted to fly out of my mouth.

Good thing Lois had told me about Firefly's peculiar attitude toward a rider's fear. He does the whole thing backwards.

In the real world, a horse picks up his rider's fear and doubles it. Panic is the usual outcome.

Firefly's different. If his rider gets scared, he takes the helm and steers the boat into calm waters. This is, I think, what Dad would call a Mixed Metaphor. Whatever that means.

Firefly doesn't panic, that's the main thing. He doesn't need to. I had enough panic for both of us.

Lois was leading the ride on an enormous bay Nancy calls The Brontosaurus. Firefly and I were right behind. Then came Birdie on Mosby, Evie on Rocket, Allie on Pocahontas and, a little behind the group, Jane on Jumping Jack Flash.

"Use a little leg, Jane, and close up the gap," Lois called over her shoulder. She turned back without seeing Jane's mutinous face.

"How are you doing, Charley? Your first trail ride with the class. It's a pretty big deal. Does it feel very different from our practice rides?"

My tongue was tied in a knot, but it didn't matter. My mouth was so dry I couldn't have spoken anyway. Lois slowed up until The Brontosaurus was walking next to Firefly, who flicked an ear in his direction and then ignored him. The horse had another name, but just at the moment I couldn't think what it was. He wasn't a school horse, that's for sure.

I managed to get enough spit together to say something. "It's okay," I croaked.

"Great," Lois said. "Then you can work on your posture and your seat."

I gave her a dirty look.

"You remember the First Principle of Horsemanship?"

We sang it out together. "'Where your eyes go your horse goes!'"

"So where're your eyes?"

"Uh, on the ground?"

I checked out my body parts. Mostly they just felt numb.

"And your legs, where are they?"

I took a quick peek. My knees were trying to crawl into my pockets. I made them relax and hang down. The stirrups got in the way, as usual, but at least I could try to look like a real rider.

"Arms? Relaxed and hanging softly by your side? Hands soft, just feeling the horse's mouth?" Lois just wouldn't quit.

"I give up! You win. Can we go home now?"

"Charley," Lois said. "Look at me. We've done this before. You can do it. You've *already* done it. Get a grip!"

I had to smile. I already had a grip. My legs were gripping Firefly like a nutcracker. His poor ribs must ache. I took a deep breath and let it out slowly.

Lois was right: I could do this.

I took another deep breath and, when I let it out, Firefly's neck relaxed some and his head came down. By my third exhale he'd even relaxed his back a little. His walk felt different. Softer. Swingier. That was better. Whew!

We walked through tall trees that filtered the light.

It wasn't dark exactly, just kind of soft and glowy. The places where sunlight broke through were so bright I had to blink. I could smell the pine trees as I swayed to the rhythm of Firefly's walk.

Then Jane screamed, and everything fell apart. We all spun around, even Firefly and me. How I stayed on I'll never know.

Jack was way behind, bucking his head off in a patch of sun. Jane was sitting in the dirt screaming and batting something away with one hand.

"Everybody stay where you are," Lois called, putting her horse into a canter. He slid to a stop, and she jumped off. Then she started waving her hands around too.

She got an arm around Jane and pulled her out of the sunlight to a shady spot in the trees.

Lois grabbed Jack's reins, remounted, and cantered back to us. She jumped off, handed the reins to Allie, and ran back to Jane. The Brontosaurus stood where she left him, his reins hanging down in front of him. A small, irrelevant voice in my head said, "So that's ground tying. Pretty impressive, huh?"

I wondered frantically what had made Jack buck like that. Could whatever it was infect Firefly, too?

Jack wasn't bucking anymore, but he was very upset. His neck was lathered up, and every time he shook his head blobs of foam flew everywhere.

Allie couldn't make him stand, so she and Pocahontas walked up and down the trail, trying to keep Jack moving so he could calm down. After what felt like an hour Lois came back carrying Jane. She wasn't screaming anymore, but her sobs made me feel sick.

The horses milled around, getting more excited every minute. Except for Firefly. He watched them make fools of themselves and turned his back.

Lois looked at each one of us and shook her head. Whatever she wanted, we didn't have it. She peeled off her shirt, folded it into a triangle, and turned it into a kind of sling for Jane's arm. Lucky it had long sleeves.

Jane's face was blotchy from crying, and there were angry red lumps on her hands and arms. Jack's belly had some lumps too, but since he was a dark bay they didn't show so much.

Firefly was the only quiet horse in the group, so I wasn't surprised when Lois asked me to dismount and seated Jane oh-so-gently in his saddle. She clipped a lead rope to his bridle and handed the looped-up end to me.

Lois led the ride back to the barn. I followed numbly, leading Firefly. Jane sobbed and hiccoughed, but didn't say a word.

Chapter Thirty

LOIS AND CAROL TOOK JANE into Fairlee for X-rays, leaving us to deal with the horses.

The aisle was crowded. Birdie and Allie untacked their horses and hosed them off. Mosby and Poco had behaved themselves—no bucking or running—but they'd caught the edge of Jack's terror and were both black with nervous sweat.

Nancy had been grooming Classic when we barged in. She put him away half done and took Jack's reins.

Poor Jack was in pitiful shape. There were welts on his legs and belly, and he trembled like a tuning fork. His face and neck were speckled with foam, and his eyes were wild.

Nancy ran the hose on his legs, moving the stream upward as he got used to the cold water. He flinched when it hit his belly, but it must have felt good. He lowered his head and started to relax. Nancy offered him little drinks of water from the hose. He drank some, but most of it went on Nancy.

For a while we played musical horses, trading spots in the wash stall for crossties in the aisle. One by one they were led outside to eat grass.

Nobody said much but we were all upset and confused. If that's what happens on trail rides, maybe I should stick to sketching horses.

I had to admit it. Firefly was pretty amazing. I might not be his favorite person, but he stayed calm, and I stayed on.

When all the horses had been fussed over and turned out in their paddocks, we were ready for a rest. Nancy and I split off the trail at Cabin One. Mercifully, it was empty.

It didn't stay empty long. I'd just gotten comfortable when Birdie plopped down on the end of my cot. She didn't look happy.

"What happened?" she asked. "We were riding along, enjoying the scenery and minding our own business. Then Jane starts to scream. Mosby's a good old boy. He held it together pretty well, but he felt like a firecracker ready to explode."

Evie came in next. She looked frazzled and scared.

"I heard Jane broke her arm and may have a fractured skull. It was supposed to be a walking trail ride! It was supposed to be short, easy, and nothing was supposed to go wrong. It was to give Charley a little confidence! Then Jane falls off, Jack has a meltdown, and even Lois's Brontosaurus loses his cool. So what went wrong?"

From Evie, who hardly ever spoke, this counted as babbling.

Nancy listened to Evie's recap of the ride and shook her head.

"Everybody calm down and be quiet. I'll try to answer your questions. First, Jane's arm *may* be broken, but the nurse thinks it's her wrist. She's gone to the hospital for X-rays. She does not have a fractured skull.

"The Brontosaurus didn't have a meltdown," she said. "He was cool as a cucumber the whole time. Here's what really happened. Lois told me all about it.

"The horses walked through a yellow jacket nest. Yellow jackets like to be warm, and they make underground nests in whatever warm places they can find. You can find them anywhere. It was bad luck the horses disturbed that nest, but there's really no way to predict something like that. Unless you only ride in indoor arenas—and where's the fun in that?"

"So why did Jack get stung and nobody else?" asked Birdie. "He wasn't doing anything, just walking along."

Nancy shrugged. "Probably the horses in front of

Jack stirred up the wasps. You have to be ready for anything."

I shook my head. How could you be ready for anything? Trying to do that would make me more nervous than I was already.

I was tired and wrung out, but a little bit proud, too. Firefly and I had kept our heads when all about us were losing theirs . . . as Dad would have said if he'd been here. I'd looked after my horse and helped everybody with theirs. When the crunch came, I hadn't been a useless fraidy-cat.

It was a relief when the bugle call for supper crackled over the loudspeaker. The day was just about done, and so was I.

Chapter Thirty-One

AFTER SUPPER WE HUNG OUT on the porch, waiting for someone to say something to make us feel better. But, really, what could anyone say?

I slipped away from the group and went to see Cricket.

I was afraid he'd be in his stall for the night, wherever that might be. He certainly didn't live in the barn with the other horses. Why not? I wondered. Horses don't like to be alone, so why was he always on his own?

I got to the fence and looked around. No Cricket. I started toward his favorite spot under the tree, tripped, and grabbed a branch to keep from falling. A black rubber saucer, big enough for a baby's bath, lay on the grass. It was so clean it shone.

I heard hoof beats behind me. Cricket trotted up, checked his dinner plate—empty—then searched me from head to knees and down the back of my shirt. Finding nothing, he went back to his grass.

Yellow Dog ghosted up and stuck her nose in my hand. It was still empty.

The sun was near to setting, but it was that soft evening time I wished would last forever. Nobody was around, not even the bugs. It was heaven.

That was the thing about camp. There was always someone nearby, someplace I had to be, something I had to do. I was getting used to it. Used to sleeping in a room full of other girls, used to getting dressed and undressed where everyone could see. Used to reading by myself in Cricket's paddock where no one could make fun of me.

It still seems bizarre to not keep a book handy in case I have five minutes with nothing to do, but people think I'm strange enough already.

I was even getting used to the food. Tonight it was mystery meat and gravy. Pardon me. At Secret Lake we call it Salisbury steak. I call it disgusting, but at least the mashed potatoes were good. And chocolate chip ice cream was the perfect way to end a perfectly awful meal.

If I could choose, I'd rather be home. Even thinking the word made my eyes tear up. I can't choose. I'm here and getting used to the whole camp thing. I'm even starting to like Firefly. He's a pretty stalwart fellow, not like poor nervous Jack.

I wondered how Jane was doing at the hospital.

A snorted breath on my neck brought me back to the here and now. Cricket had been chewing on mint, or maybe he'd just rolled in some. He smelled like Wrigley's spearmint gum. It was a pity Yellow Dog hadn't rolled in it, too. She smelled like dead rat. *Ee-yew*. No kisses for Yellow Dog tonight.

I sat down under the tree and leaned against the trunk. Tomorrow was another riding lesson. I had no idea what Lois had planned. I hoped it wasn't another trail ride, but I didn't have the energy to worry.

Ouch!

I jumped up and batted at my neck, trying to knock away whatever was biting me. A big black ant fell onto my arm. I smacked it, but there were more. I spun around to look at the tree trunk. Lots and lots of big black ants. I'd been leaning against an ant highway, and they'd just turned me into a detour.

I took off my T-shirt and wadded it up to scrub ants off my neck and arms. Cricket and Yellow Dog watched me carefully from a safe distance. I shook dead ants out of my shirt and put it back on.

It was time to head back. In a few minutes it would be too dark to find my way.

THE CABIN WAS CROWDED. JANE'S wrist was wrapped in a tight elastic bandage and the tips of her fingers were blue. Her lips were bluish, too.

Everyone was talking at once. Everyone except Jane. She sat still and looked like she wanted to lie down.

Carol walked in and the talking stopped.

"There's good news and not so good news. Jane has sprained her wrist. The good news is, it will heal fast. The bad news is, sprains often hurt more than broken bones. More nerve endings.

"It's time to get ready for bed. Cabin One girls, grab your stuff and go to the noss. Everybody else, out!" She ignored the chorus of protests, standing her ground at the cabin door. "Get a move on. Jane is tired and her wrist hurts. Even if you don't need to sleep, she does. Ten minutes to lights out."

"But taps isn't until nine-thirty," yelled Debbie. "We still have twenty minutes!"

"Not tonight, you don't. Bed! Pronto! No backtalk."

Lying in bed, wide awake, I kept seeing Jack buck and Jane on the ground screaming. It was like watching a movie. I thought about how scared she must have been and how much her wrist must hurt.

In my dreams it was me on the ground screaming.

Chapter Thirty-Two

"Now the day is over,

Night is drawing nigh;

Shadows of the evening

Steal across the sky. . . ."

THE LAST NOTES DISAPPEARED LIKE wisps of smoke from a campfire just starting to catch.

Leaning back against a pine tree, full of pizza and brownies, not even tomorrow's lesson could shake my feeling of peace. I love this time of night. I love sitting around the fire. I even liked the song.

Maybe it was time to go home before I turned into a werewolf.

Mrs. Behrens walked into the circle and held a long match to the kindling.

"Thank you, Stella, the fire looks just perfect.

"We have a special visitor tonight, someone who has probably forgotten more about horses than most of us will ever learn. I would like to introduce the extraordinary horsewoman who founded Secret Lake Camp and made it what it is today: Mrs. Ethel Calhoun, my grandmother."

We all clapped politely. Nancy leaned over and whispered, "I thought she was dead!"

"Shhhh!" Birdie whispered, loudly enough to be heard back in the barn.

A gray-haired old lady, straight-backed and severe, walked slowly to the edge of the circle. Annette brought over a chair and held it while she sat down and propped her cane against the chair.

Was this the woman people whispered about? I guess Cricket didn't kill her after all.

"Good evening, girls. I'll bet you're wondering why I've come back from the dead to speak with you tonight."

A tiny smile quirked up her lips as she nodded to Nancy, who looked like she wanted to die herself.

"I heard there was an upsetting episode on a trail ride this week. To help you understand it, I thought I'd share with you a few things I've learned about horses over the years.

"For many of you"—she nodded at the group of seniors clumped across the circle—"this will be old news, but it never hurts to be reminded how the equine brain works. And for those new to riding, these few facts might help you avoid, or at least understand, some painful, embarrassing, and often dangerous situations."

She looked across at Jane, the only camper sitting in a chair. Her face was so angry it might have frozen that way.

"So. Let's start, shall we?

"We all love horses. That's why we're here, correct?" Mrs. Calhoun smiled. "We love our horses, and our horses love us. That's true enough . . . except when it isn't.

"It's the times when it isn't, and why, that I want to talk about.

"If I were to ask you to tell me about horses, I can make a list in advance of some of the things you would say. 'They are beautiful, sweet, majestic, fleet as the wind.' And so they are. But what's the number one characteristic everyone involved with horses absolutely must understand?

"Anyone?"

A pine cone dropped, exploding in the silence.

"Horses are stupid. Really, really stupid.

"I know this isn't what you want to hear about the horses you love, but it's true, and it's important. They're stupid and easily frightened. And when they're frightened, they run. Mostly. Sometimes they rear, or kick, or buck."

Someone across the fire whispered loudly, "And sometimes they crash."

Mrs. Calhoun looked confused for a second, then continued.

"One other thing, maybe two, and then s'mores and cocoa. Horses evolved as prey animals. They lived in herds for protection and depended on one another to keep watch for wolves and mountain lions—maybe even saber-toothed cats. They also kept a lookout for us. Humans hunted horses long before we rode them. We hunted them and—when we were lucky in the hunt—we ate them."

A chorus of *no way* and *yuck* rippled around the circle.

She smiled and kept talking. "These days horses live in barns. We feed them. We care for them. We train them to trust us. We love them with all our hearts. And we forget—and mostly they forget—that deep in the memory of their brains and bodies, we humans are scary and dangerous. We are top predators. They are prey. We want to eat them.

"So sometimes, when a horse gets frightened, his rider can't calm him down just by being there. Just being there is part of what is scaring the horse.

"What can we do to help the horse calm down? That's a whole big subject in itself, but I can give you a hint: We can let the horse do what he wants to do when he's scared. We can let him move.

"That's what Allie did when she ponied Jack after he was stung by the wasps. She didn't let him run, which he'd have loved to do. She kept him walking up and down the road. A frightened horse can't stand still, and Allie didn't try to make him. She let him move, but at the pace she chose. She made him walk."

I wondered if it would be all right to interrupt. There were things I needed to know.

Why was Firefly so calm? Why didn't the other horses get scared and run away? Could Jane have stopped Jack from bucking her off?

Just like horses when they're scared, I was having trouble sitting still. I wanted to move!

I counted to ten, stood up, and raised my hand.

Chapter Thirty-Three

Dear Sally,

It's been quite a week. The group trail ride was supposed to be a big nothing, just half an hour's walk with a few experienced riders and calm horses. I don't need to tell you it didn't work out that way.

Jane's horse got stung by yellow jackets and bucked her off. Everyone was so upset there was a special Campfire about it.

After dinner the owner's grandmother gave us a talk on horse psychology, all about what scaredy-cats horses are and how they never totally trust us humans to keep them safe.

I don't know so many horses personally, but the two I do know, Firefly and Cricket, don't seem to be like that. Firefly is a real stalwart. Nothing fazes him, except maybe me flopping around on his back when I try to post. He took care of me when everyone else, horses and riders both, seemed to be losing their minds.

And Cricket? He's so calm and funny. It's hard to imagine anything scaring him.

So while this old woman, Mrs. Calhoun, was speaking, I got more and more uncomfortable. What good was all this talking if it didn't make sense of what the horses actually did on the trail ride?

Finally, I did something I never do. I put my hand up and interrupted the talk. Everyone was surprised, including me.

I was scared and wanted answers. Why was Firefly brave and Jack was not? And the other horses—Mosby, Pocahontas and Rocket—why did they keep listening to their riders even though they were upset?

Could Jane have done something to keep Jack from bucking her off?

You could have heard a pin drop. Even the crickets stopped sawing at their violins. My face burst into flames, but I didn't back off. If I'm going to ride, I have to know how to keep safe.

Mrs. Calhoun burst out laughing! "Great questions," she said. "There are two quick answers here that are really two sides of the same coin."

The breath I'd been holding eased out of my lungs, and I sat back down.

"The first answer is 'knowledge is power.' The more you know, the more ways you have of staying one step ahead of your horse. This refers to human beings.

"The second is 'horses are horses.' They aren't dogs, or bicycles, or automobiles. They are living, breathing creatures with minds of their own. The more we can learn about what horses are and why they are that way, the better chance we have of not getting hurt."

Mrs. Calhoun looked around at all of us, like she was weighing us up, and smiled an evil smile. "That's why horses are more fun—and more dangerous—than bicycles."

She's going to give some talks to anyone who wants to learn about horse psychology. I'm not sure I want to go. The more I hear about how frightened horses can get, the more frightened I get. And believe me, I'm scared enough already.

Then she did the weirdest thing. She looked me straight in the eye and said quietly, "So you're Charley. You and I will talk soon."

I nearly wet my pants.

Love,
Charley

Chapter Thirty-Four

RAIN THUNDERED ON THE ROOF. It was going to be a dreary, boring day. No swimming, no canoeing, no archery. Just arts and crafts (ugh!), drama, and free periods to do what we want.

I could always reread *Born to Trot*, or maybe work on the sketch of Cricket I'd started, but I didn't feel like doing anything. Except maybe starting a fight with Jane. Now that would be fun! I lay down on my cot to think how the fight might go.

When Carol came into the cabin calling my name, I woke up. She handed me a note and gave me some space to read it.

"Dear Charley," I read. "It's a terrible day, and I crave some company. Please visit this afternoon at two o'clock. I make decent hot chocolate, and if that's not inducement enough, we can talk about the horse you call Cricket.

Your creaky old friend,

Ethel Calhoun

Regrets Only."

Wow! Mrs. Calhoun wasn't kidding when she said we'd meet again soon. Did I want to go? Maybe not, but the chance to find out about Cricket was too good to pass up. I stood up and looked for Carol. She was on the porch leaning on a furled umbrella, reading her mail.

"How do I say yes?" I asked.

She took a quick look at the note and pointed to the last line. "It says Regrets Only. You don't need to reply if you want to go."

It sounded like the best offer I was going to get today.

THE RAIN SHEETED DOWN AS I slogged to Mrs. Calhoun's house. Without Carol's umbrella I'd probably have drowned.

The door was open. Mrs. Calhoun sat at the window with her cane by her side and a plate of something that smelled awfully good on the small round table in front of her. I shook rain off the umbrella and leaned it against the house.

"Hello, Charley. Come in and sit down."

The chair was hard and very upright. I didn't know

where to put my feet. She poured two cups of cocoa and handed me a plate full of . . . meringues. My favorite cookie.

"Well, go on, child, have one. They're my speciality."

The meringue was crunchy and a little bit chewy, then soft and melty on the inside. They tasted just like my mother's. I swallowed, took a sip of chocolate, and leaned back in the chair.

"Thank you, Mrs. Calhoun," I said. "The meringues are delicious."

"Call me Ethel, please. No need to make me feel even older than I am."

It didn't seem right to call someone old enough be my great-grandmother by her first name, so I didn't call her anything.

"Carol called him Promise. Is that his real name?"

Ethel turned to look out at the rain. "Actually," she answered, "his real name is Broken Promise. It's a long story."

She offered the plate and I took another meringue. Chewing saved me from having to talk.

"For today, let's call him Cricket," she said. "It's a good name for a very good little horse."

"Why is he always by himself? I thought horses hated being alone."

"That's another story," Ethel said.

I could see we were getting nowhere. Maybe I should just shut up and let her talk. Another meringue disappeared practically crumb by crumb.

"How did you come to meet him?"

"Cricket? Kind of by accident. It was right after my first lesson on Firefly. My first lesson on anyone. My first time on a horse."

Ethel kept looking out the window. It was still raining.

"I didn't even manage to get into the saddle. Every time I tried, he moved away."

A tiny smile crept onto Ethel's face.

"It wasn't funny! He didn't want me on his back? Fine. I didn't want to be there either. I ran back to the cabin, but I was so busy running I went right past it and ended up at Cricket's field."

"Ah."

"He came over to see me. He blew in my nostrils! When I left, he didn't want me to go."

"He's a lover, that one."

I beamed. I couldn't help myself. "It's like he really wanted to be friends."

"In all my years," Ethel said, "I've never met a more

charming horse. Even people who don't like horses can't resist him."

Did that mean I wasn't special? That he didn't love me best? I wasn't so happy about that.

"He's a Morgan." My heart fluttered as she said it. "They're quite different from other breeds. Some people call them the Labrador Retrievers of the horse world and think they'll love just anyone. It's not so. Morgans are very discriminating. They pick and they choose. When Cricket picked you, he knew what he was doing."

Her eyes went back to the window. The rain was stopping. Maybe we'd have some fun today after all.

"I've been in love with horses all my life," she said softly. "I've worked with hundreds, bred quite a few, had a lot of successes and more failures than I'd like. I've never known a horse quite like Promise—or Cricket, if you prefer. He's such a complex character. Whenever I thought I had him figured out, he'd do something to surprise me."

That sounded good. "Can you tell me about him? Some stories, maybe?"

"Hmm. You asked why he isn't with the other horses in the big barn. There are two answers to that question. First, for ten months of the year, Secret Lake is a boarding establishment. People pay to have their horses live here. Cricket isn't a boarder, and he can sometimes cause trouble for his stable mates."

"What kind of trouble?" I was bouncing in my seat just like Sally.

"Well, for one thing, he's an escape artist. An absolute genius at opening doors, gates—anything that keeps him from where he wants to go. I've never seen him do it, but he's gotten out of every kind of enclosure we have. I finally started closing his stall door with bungee cords. Even he can't open one of those."

"What's the other thing he does?"

"He leads jail breaks."

Huh?

"It's bad enough that he lets himself out. Then he lets other horses out to keep him company. For a time I bungeed every stall door closed. Then I moved Cricket out of the barn altogether. That spoiled his fun. It's been ages since he opened a gate."

"But he's all alone. That can't be good."

"He's not alone. Haven't you met Sunshine? She's a yellow lab who spends most of her time in the field with him.

"It's not uncommon for solitary horses to adopt animal companions. Cricket's sire, Applevale El

Supremo, spent a lot of time in a stall. He had a cat for a best friend. The cat lived in the barn and did what barn cats do—catch mice and rats. She spent hours every day with El Supremo, sleeping in his hay crib or cuddled up against his tummy in the straw."

"I've seen Cricket do that!" I said. "He was asleep on the ground, and a yellow dog was sleeping right up against him. From a distance it looked like a banana!" I thought about that scene. Cricket and Yellow Dog certainly seemed to be a team. "When Cricket colicked, Yellow Dog came and got me. She made me go to Cricket's field. . . .

"Tell me some more," I added. "What does he like to do?"

Ethel nodded. "It's easier to tell you what he doesn't like. He's a dominant horse who doesn't like to be schooled. Once he gets something right he wants to move on and try something new. He doesn't like being bossed around, either. A 51-49% human-horse split suits him best. He'll give you the two percentage points unless he feels you're wrong. Then he'll do it his way.

"He's insatiably curious. One morning when I came down to feed, he looked like Santa Claus. He had a white beard about three inches long all over his muzzle. Mr. Curious had tried to investigate a porcupine.

"He was sensible about it. The quills must have been painful, but he didn't panic. He just waited for me to save him. The vet came and tranked him, then pulled out each quill with pliers. Promise—Cricket— just stood there, swaying a little from the drug, and rested his head on my shoulder with his chin hanging over so the vet could get at his poor nose."

"Is he nice to ride?"

"He's awful. He never liked being sat upon. He'd stiffen his neck and pull like a train. If I didn't wear gloves, he'd give me blisters. Sometimes he'd even get light in front, which is totally unacceptable."

"What's 'light in front'?"

"He'd threaten to rear. Horses who rear as a way to get out of work have a tendency to go over backwards. So no riding for Himself. He had to do something, so I taught him to drive."

"To drive what?" I asked stupidly. A vision of a small black horse driving a snazzy red convertible played on my movie screen.

"I had a little two-wheeled road cart. I taught him to drive that. Driving, he liked."

Ethel looked out the window for so long I thought maybe I'd lost her again. She turned back and smiled. "Sun's out. Go on back to camp. It's almost time for free swim."

Before I could get through the door, Ethel called me back.

"I want to thank you for looking after Promise when he had colic. I know it was a long, hard, and scary time but, believe me, you saved the day."

Well, okay, but why isn't someone keeping an eye on him?

I didn't say it. What was the point? But I thought it as loudly as I could.

Yellow Dog was waiting for me on the front steps. We took a detour on the way back to say hello to Cricket.

Chapter Thirty-Five

IT WAS REST HOUR. I pulled some writing paper out of my trunk and sat cross-legged on the floor, using the trunk as a desk.

Dear Mom and Dad,

I'm having a problem at camp. It's this cough. I'm fine all day—but as soon as I go to bed I start to cough.

It's not a big cough, not full of mucus or anything gross, but it starts when I lie down and just doesn't stop.

I've tried holding my breath when I feel one coming, or clenching my teeth. I've rolled on my side and buried my face in the pillow. Nothing helps. I just keep coughing.

I even went to the nurse. Carol made me. I had to lean over a bowl of boiling water with a big towel over my head so I could breathe in the steam. It smelled like mint and camph—

A hand came over my left shoulder and snatched the letter. I jumped to my feet, ready for a fight. Jane held it up and made a big deal of reading it out loud to her two henchmen.

I grabbed for the letter and hung on. It tore in half, and she wadded up her half and threw it on the floor. I picked it up and tried to smooth out the crinkles.

"There's something seriously wrong with you," Jane said. "All that coughing. Maybe it's really catching, like TD."

She turned to Pam and Debbie. "They shouldn't let her stay. We could all get sick."

"What's TD?" Debbie asked.

"You know, it's this lung thing that kills people in Africa. You catch it from mosquitoes. It's horribly contagious." Jane smiled her know-it-all smile.

Birdie walked into the cabin. "Close, but no cigar!" She examined Jane from head to toe. "I take it back," she added. "You're not even close."

Jane looked confused.

"Never mind," said Birdie. "One of these days you'll learn how to read."

She glanced at me. "Ready?"

I grabbed my towel, and we were out the door.

We headed for the lake to sign out a canoe.

"What bone was *she* gnawing on?" Birdie asked.

"Jane's leading a delegation to get me kicked out. She said I shouldn't be allowed to infect everyone." I brightened up a little. "Do you think they'll send me home?"

Birdie frowned. "You still want to go home? I thought you were starting to like it here. Anyway, you can't leave. I need you. You're the only one who gets my jokes."

"What if I actually have TD?" I concentrated on the stones in the path and tried to step on every fourth one.

"You mean the cough you get from mosquito bites that kills a lot of people in Africa? Jane's been watching too much television. Or maybe she reads the magazines in the checkout lines at the supermarket. She means TB—tuberculosis. You don't get it from mosquitoes, you get it from germs. TB is a lung disease, but trust me. You don't have it."

"How do you know? I cough a lot, every night."

We paddled to the middle of the lake and just floated. Out of touch with everyone, I could feel myself quieting down inside. The lake was like glass, no wind, not even a ripple.

"My oldest brother has asthma," Birdie said. "He takes pills now, but before we found out what it was, he coughed all the time. We never figured out what he was allergic to. Probably everything. That's the kind of boy he is."

"I'm allergic to a bunch of things, but mostly my nose gets stuffed up and I can't breathe through it. It doesn't make me cough."

Birdie shrugged. "You're probably allergic to Jane. I know I would be. She's the most irritating person I ever met."

Chapter Thirty-Six

WHEN I WALKED BACK THROUGH the cabin door, everything felt different. Jane and her two drones were tackling Evie and Nancy.

"She really shouldn't be living with us," Debbie said to Evie. "She's keeping us awake, and nobody knows what's wrong with her. What if it's really, you know, catching? We could all get sick, and the whole summer would be ruined."

Jane was hissing at Nancy. ". . . know I'm right. She can't just move in here and wreck our whole summer. If she's sick she should go home. This is Camp, not a charitable institution."

"A what?" Nancy sounded frazzled, which she hardly ever did.

"A place where people can come for free. Like a welfare hospital. We're here to ride, not risk our lives sleeping with Typhoid Mary."

Maybe the cough really could get me out of here!

But, when it came right down to it, I didn't want to

go. At home there were no horses. At camp I had Cricket and even—in a weird sort of way—Firefly. He might not like me much, but he was beginning to make me like him.

Jane was backing Nancy into a corner. "Can you sleep with all that racket? Nobody else can. Charley should be sleeping somewhere else."

Carol opened the door, and everybody shut up. Fast. Then they all started talking at once.

"One at a time! Nancy, you start. What's happening here?"

"Some of the kids think Charley's cough could be contagious. They want her to go home."

Carol gave Jane a long, cold stare. What my mother would call an "old-fashioned look." What made it old-fashioned I had no idea, but it pinned Jane to the wall. Being Jane, she didn't stay pinned.

"Why should we risk our summer if she has something we could catch? If she won't go home, she should move to the infirmary. Let the nurse figure it out."

"Then maybe we could get some sleep!" This was from Pam, who rarely said anything.

"Evie?" Carol asked. "Do you think Charley should go home?" Poor Evie. She turned beet red and stared at the floor. "Evie?" Carol asked again.

"No," Evie whispered. "I want her to stay."

"What about the noise?"

Evie's face got even redder.

"It's hard to sleep," she said softly. "But it's not Charley's fault. She tries to stop coughing, but it doesn't work."

"See?" Jane grinned, and then pounced. "Cough, cough, cough. Nobody can sleep."

"Come on, Charley." Carol opened the door. "Let's take a walk."

Chapter Thirty-Seven

EXCEPT FOR ME, THE INFIRMARY was empty.

It was a big white room, and even at this late hour it held the light. I looked out the window. No pine trees to block the sun. Three white iron beds, all made up with white sheets and green blankets, were lined up against the wall. The room was spotless. It even *smelled* clean.

A young-looking woman with sandy blonde hair and a white uniform walked through the door. "My name's Marie," she said. Take any bed you want. You're my only customer tonight."

After arranging my sketch pad, pencils, and a couple of books on the night table, I put on my pj's, brushed my teeth, and washed my face. Then there was nothing to do but get into bed.

I waited for the coughing to start but it didn't. How embarrassing would it be if I really *was* allergic to my cabin! Or maybe Birdie was right and I was allergic to Jane.

Nurse Marie leaned over to feel my forehead, then put her lips against one temple.

"You don't feel feverish," she said, "but it never hurts to be sure. Open up."

She stuck a thermometer under my tongue, and I started to cough. It came like an avalanche, a force of nature. I couldn't get my breath. Then I thought about all those poor Africans getting TD from mosquitoes, and I started to laugh.

Soon I was crying so hard I didn't have the breath to laugh. The more I cried, the worse it got, like a tidal wave coming to wash me away. Like Alice drowning in her tears.

Nothing Nurse Marie tried helped at all. Finally she just put her arms around me and rocked back and forth, humming some kind of song under her breath.

WHEN I WOKE UP SUN was shining through the big windows, and Ethel was sitting next to my bed reading. She'd brought a satchel for my things and clean clothes from my trunk.

There was a full water glass on the nightstand. I emptied it so fast I choked.

"Does that feel a little better? You must be perishing

with thirst."

She refilled the glass. I grabbed it and drank about half before my stomach started to rebel. I thought I might puke all over Ethel's shoes.

"Deep breaths," she said quietly. "Breathe in, count to three; breathe out, count to three. You're not going to throw up." She smiled. "You certainly look green, though. I don't think I've ever seen skin quite that color."

Breathing like she said, I looked out the window. In a minute my stomach was okay. My clothes were on the straight chair near the bed. I picked them up and looked at Ethel. What was I supposed to do now?

"Get dressed, Charley. I'm taking you home with me. After breakfast we'll start sorting out this cough of yours."

In the bathroom I peed, washed my hands, and brushed my teeth, then splashed my face with water so cold it tingled. The front of my pajama top was soaked. I crumpled my pj's into a ball and put on clean shorts and a shirt.

Ethel's little bag was already packed. She took the pajamas from my hand, wrapped them in a towel, and laid them on top of the bag. Nurse Marie waved goodbye, and we walked out of the infirmary into a soft and sunny morning.

Chapter Thirty-Eight

THE HOUSE SEEMED VERY FAR away. We walked slowly because that's how Ethel walks. She carried her cane but didn't use it. For the hundredth time I wondered why she carried it at all.

In the kitchen, Ethel put the kettle on for tea.

"How long have you been coughing, Charley?"

I shrugged, trying to remember.

She squeezed a lemon into a mug, then added hot water and a big spoonful of honey. She handed me the mug and sat down.

"Sip that slowly and see if it helps. Your throat is probably sore from last night. When did the coughing start? Did it come on suddenly or sneak up when you weren't looking?"

I blew on the tea and thought back.

"It snuck up on me. Every once in a while I'd cough, mostly in the late afternoon when the air starts to cool off. But it wasn't much. Just a few minutes, then it was gone. It got bad during movie night last week. I started coughing and couldn't stop. I ended up sitting outside on the deck while the movie finished."

"What movie was it?"

"*The Black Stallion and Satan.* The book's on my shelf at home, but I hadn't seen the movie. It was a drag having to leave but everyone was staring."

"Then what?"

I tried to remember. When did I start coughing for real?

"I think it was after we started talking about Parents' Weekend. I still don't know if my parents are coming."

I could feel a black cloud settle on my shoulders. It weighed a ton and had a bitter smell that caught in my throat. I started coughing again.

Ethel made more tea, adding a tablespoon of apple cider vinegar to the honey and lemon. She talked about herbal teas and how they've been used for hundreds of years, but I didn't listen. I wanted to be home—with Mom and Dad and Jeremy and everything back to the way it was. I gritted my teeth and tried to stop coughing.

The hot drink took the sting out of the back of my throat, and the cough slowly went away. I sat in Ethel's kitchen and stared at the floor, totally wrung out.

She paid no attention, just put together the batter for blueberry pancakes as if nothing was wrong. Ethel pointed to the silverware drawer.

I swallowed a sigh, the kind that drives my mother crazy, and set the table.

The pancakes tasted like cardboard. I pushed them around my plate and hid pieces under my knife and fork.

"Tell me about Parents' Weekend. It's usually a happy time for the campers. They love showing off their new skills to impress Mom and Dad. Why is it making you so unhappy?"

I looked at the floor some more. "I don't know if they're coming. I don't know if they're even speaking to each other. Dad's moved out. Unless their letters come from both of them, I won't answer, so they stopped writing."

My eyes filled with tears, and I clenched my teeth to keep them back.

"Then I wrote to tell them to come to Parents' Weekend together or stay home. I think they're going to stay home." A tear slid down my cheek into my mouth. "It's not fair! Why do they have to get a divorce? Why can't they just work it out! Everybody else's parents stay married. Why can't mine?"

I started to cough again. It was the last straw.

Ethel carried our dishes to the sink. She put my plate on the floor for the cat to finish.

Do cats eat blueberry pancakes? This one took a sniff and went back to wherever it had been sleeping.

Chapter Thirty-Nine

THE TREES DRIPPED. THE CABINS dripped. It was too hot to move.

I stopped at Cabin Three to collect Birdie, and we trudged to the canoe dock, slower than snails.

We should have trudged faster.

Jane materialized on the path and blocked it.

Oh, God, I thought. What now?

"How's your cough?" Jane asked, with a curl of her lip. "Infected anyone lately?"

Birdie moved in front of me and stared at Jane's mouth until she licked her lips and backed up. Good trick, I thought. I bet she has dogs at home. Maybe I should try it on Yellow Dog.

"How's life at the Calhoun residence? All comfy and cozy? Learned any good secrets lately?"

"Secrets?" I asked stupidly.

"Spit it out," Birdie said, looking toward the lake. "Spit it out or skip it. We don't have time for your idiocy." She looked at me. "Let's go."

"Wait a sec," Jane said. "There's more to your precious Ethel than you think. Why does she hide in that house of hers? Why does she carry that stupid cane?"

She took a breath. "Why did Nancy think she was *dead*?"

Birdie shouldered her way past Jane, pushing her off the path. "Time to hit the lake and cool off."

We signed out a canoe and paddled to the middle of Secret Lake. The silence fell on my shoulders like a cool towel.

"What do you think she meant?" Birdie asked. "Did Nancy really think Mrs. Calhoun was dead?"

I shrugged. Nancy knew a lot more about Secret Lake than I did.

"It is strange, though," I said. "Maybe I'll ask her about it. Or maybe not. It doesn't have anything to do with me."

Chapter Forty

I COULDN'T STOP CRYING. IT was all I seemed to do these days.

Ethel sat in her chair and looked out the window. She finally left the room and came back with a damp washcloth.

"Mop up with this, Charley. I have a surprise for you."

What kind of surprise? I couldn't guess, but just sitting there with snot dripping down my face was getting me exactly nowhere. I walked to the bathroom and turned the cold tap on all the way.

When I got back to the living room, Ethel was waiting for me at the door.

We headed towards Cricket's field. I ran ahead to give him a private hug. He snuffled my hair and gave a little shove with his shoulder. "Buck up," he seemed to be saying. I immediately felt better.

Ethel took his halter from its place on the fence. Cricket came over, shoved his nose in her face, and exhaled loudly. It was like he was saying hello after a long separation.

"Come on, Promise," she said. "Let's go for a walk."

She clipped on his lead rope and handed it to me. We started walking slowly towards the barn. Ethel led the way right past Firefly's barn to where the boarders live. It was out of bounds for campers, and I'd never been inside.

"Put him in the crossties," Ethel said, "and give him a good brush. I'll get his harness ready to go."

Harness? Cricket? My heart started to zing around in my chest. I grabbed a grooming bucket and went to work.

By the time I was brushing away the last of the dust, Ethel was back with her arms full of leather. She arranged the pieces on a hook hanging in the aisle. It was really three hooks in one and, when Ethel started loading it up, I could see why. She separated the pieces of harness and hung them neatly on the hooks.

It looked to be a lot to put on one little horse.

Ethel assembled the harness with Cricket on the inside, and I tried to make sense of what she was doing. It was nothing like tacking up a horse to ride. I hoped she knew what she was doing, because I was totally confused.

Once the pieces of harness were in place and all buckled up, Ethel took his halter off and picked up the bridle.

She offered Cricket the bit, and he gave her a death stare. Ethel stared right back until he sighed, opened his mouth a little, and accepted the bit. She eased the bridle over his ears, buckled the throatlatch, and attached incredibly long reins to the rings on each side of the bit.

"Lines," Ethel said. "Not reins."

She fed the lines through two sets of brass rings ("keepers," she called them), coiled them neatly, and laid them on the seat. Then Ethel put his halter on over the bridle and handed the lead rope to me.

"Take him outside and stand him up in front of the carriage," she said.

It was the cutest thing I'd ever seen. The body of the cart was dark green with gold accents and racing stripes, and two big green-and-gold wheels. It leaned against the ground on two long painted shafts with brass caps on the ends. In the front of the cart was a snazzy brass and patent leather dashboard.

The seat was black, with a rim about four inches high around the back—not tall enough to lean on, but maybe enough to keep a person from falling out backwards. On each side was a little round step for getting in, and black arm-resty things that I guessed might keep you from falling out sideways.

Why was I thinking about falling out? It couldn't be dangerous or Ethel wouldn't be doing it.

"Just head him while I hitch," Ethel said. "The point is to keep him from moving off with the hitching half done."

She fussed with the cart and harness, muttering to herself as she worked. Cricket stood with one hind foot cocked, eyes half closed. He looked like he was falling asleep.

When he was standing between the shafts, and about a hundred different straps and buckles had been done up, horse and cart were totally connected. Ethel went over the harnessing again, checking things off as she went. *Tugs, traces, wrap girth, breeching.* It all sounded like gobbledy-gook.

After a really long time she turned to face me.

"Take off his halter, Charley. If he starts to move, hold the lines right near the bit and tell him to stand. This is the trickiest part of driving—getting in the cart. If he walks off while I'm getting in, well, it could be trouble. Promise was a bugger about standing when he was young, but he's an old man now, and I hope for better things."

Ethel picked up the lines and put her left foot on the cart's round step. With a little hop and a pivot, she got in and settled on the seat. Then she arranged the lines in her lap, picked up the long black whip, and turned to me.

"Do what I did," she said. "Left foot on the step and hop up."

It was easier said than done. In fact it wasn't easy at all. I was too nervous to figure out which foot was my left. Then, when I had the right—I mean left—foot on the step, I couldn't work out how to hop up without facing backwards. I had to replay the film in my head several times before I had a clear view of the move.

Up in the cart, facing the right way, I felt completely wrung out. I snuck a look at Ethel. She was laughing.

"I told you it was tricky," she said, trying to swallow her smile. "But you're in now, safe and sound."

Chapter Forty-One

ETHEL REARRANGED THE LINES, LOOKED at the whip in her right hand and put it back in its holder. Then she took a deep breath, taking forever to let it out. She gave a funny little shiver, leaned back and said, "Promise, walk up."

Cricket gave the same little shake that Ethel did, snorted, and began to walk.

"I haven't driven in a long time," Ethel said, "so I had my granddaughter take him out for a spin just to remind him what is required of a well-trained, well-mannered carriage horse. Not that his manners were ever all that good."

She laughed, but it wasn't her normal laugh. It sounded strangled.

Ethel steered him past the cabins and the noss and turned into the woods on a dirt road I hadn't noticed before. It was wider than the trail where the wasps were, and smooth, except for where something heavy had made ruts in the road. Ethel kept away from the ruts and we walked along, not saying anything.

I was entranced by this view of Cricket. When you ride, you can only see from his shoulders and up his neck to where his ears stick up. Now I could see all of him except for the front of his face. I liked watching his butt and tail sway as he walked. It was very relaxing.

I glanced at Ethel, who did not look very relaxed.

"A carriage horse has to have a good, solid walk," she said. "If you have to struggle to keep a horse in the walk, it's very trying. Poor Promise hated to walk. He was bred to be a park harness horse, and, if you asked him, he'd say he was born to trot.

"My daughter taught him to drive and had the devil of a time teaching him the flat-footed walk. The more she tried, the more uppity he'd be. In desperation, she started singing to him. He loves music, and I guess the singing distracted him enough to let him walk like a normal horse."

The more she talked the tighter her voice got. Cricket's head was getting higher and tighter, too. Maybe I should sing and calm them both down.

We came out of the woods into bright sunlight. The barn in the distance looked a million miles away. Cricket pricked his ears and broke into a trot.

Ethel froze. Her face was as rigid as a stone carving,

and her hands held the lines in a death grip. Cricket trotted faster. Ethel just sat there, hanging onto the lines like she was drowning.

The words of her campfire talk came to me in a flash of understanding:

When you're frightened, it frightens the horse. They are herd animals, and in every herd someone has to be the boss. If you can't lead, the horse will—and horses, compared to humans, are incredibly stupid. Their first response to fear is to run. So if it's just you and the horse, you have to step up and lead.

Ethel sure looked to be afraid, and I wasn't far behind. If I didn't do something, we would have a train wreck.

I couldn't take the lines. Even if I could, what would I do with them? By the time I got them organized we'd be in a ditch. I looked down at Ethel's hands with their bony white knuckles, and put mine over her cold ones. I didn't have the lines, but I could move her hands closer to her belly and maybe slow Cricket down before it was too late.

"Easy, Cricky-boy," I crooned, moving Ethel's fists back and forth. "Just slow down and take it easy. You know me, and you know I won't let anything bad happen. Just slo-o-ow do-o-wn."

His ears flicked back to listen and his head went down a fraction. I kept talking nonsense, anything that came to mind. Then I started to sing.

"Aah-ji boo, aah-ji boo, aah-ji aah-ji, aah-ji, aah-ji boo boo boo. . . ."

My mother used to sing that to me when I had a bad dream. Stupid, I know, but I didn't have time to go through the hit parade looking for a tune!

I kept talking to Cricket, telling him what a good boy he was, and how nice it was to slow down and walk.

"Walking's good. You don't get tired and the cart slows down. Everything's okay. Everything's fine. It's me, Charley, and I need you to slow down and walk."

When words failed I went back to the dumb little lullaby and sang for a minute or two. Cricket's head sank lower and his trot became slower and slower. I finally said the magic words.

"Walk, please. And whoa."

I didn't think it would work, but it did.

I sat in the cart, holding Ethel's shaking hands, for what seemed like a long time. Mine were shaking, too. Pretty soon my whole body was shaking. I didn't feel scared, but I was cold and couldn't stop shivering.

Ethel took in a big breath and seemed to wake up. She looked at me, blinked, and looked again.

"Charley? Are you all right?"

I didn't know what to say. Was I? Well, I wasn't dead, so I nodded. Ethel nodded back, and we sat there, like two dummies, not saying anything.

Finally, she took control of the lines again and turned to me.

"I want you to get out of the cart backwards, Charley, then stand in front of Promise like you did before. If he tries to move away you can hold the lines, but I'll bet you won't need to."

Getting down was harder than it looked.

"Pivot around like you're going down a ladder and put your right foot on the little step. You should be able to get the other foot onto the ground from there. You can hold on to the side of the cart for balance."

I scrambled out of the cart and managed not to fall over. Standing at Cricket's head, I blew into his nostrils. Then I hugged him around the neck, hard. He was a little sweaty, but otherwise looked as calm as could be.

"All in a day's work, hey, Cricket? Thanks for stopping. I didn't know what I was doing." He blew a big spitty breath right in my face. "Thanks a lot," I said, wiping my face on my sleeve. I leaned against his neck and breathed in his sweet horsey smell.

"I'm coming down now, Charley. It would be good

if Promise didn't move. I'm not as nimble as I used to be."

Ethel bunched the lines into one hand and got out of the cart much more gracefully than I had. Cricket didn't move a muscle. I kissed the side of his nose to say thank you.

"Why don't you lead him back to the barn while I get my breath back. You two can wait for me in front of the big door where we hitched up."

I wasn't quite sure where she meant, but it didn't matter. Cricket knew.

We made it almost to the barn door before I threw up.

AFTERWARDS, I SAT IN ETHEL'S living room with a cup of herbal tea, watching her look more and more uncomfortable. Her face was gray and, for the first time since I'd known her, she looked . . . old.

I didn't know how to help her.

Finally, she squared her shoulders and began to talk.

"Charley," she started. "I'm sorry your first carriage ride had such an unexpected ending. It's been years since I've driven, but I truly thought it was like riding a bike. Once you know how, you never forget.

"I didn't expect all the memories it would dredge up. I didn't expect to be flooded with fear.

"Your fear of riding is in the here and now. The more you learn, the more confident you'll become.

"Mine comes from long ago, from something that happened when I was driving. I haven't thought about it in years. I thought it would stay in the past."

Her face got even more strained and tired.

"I should have known. At the very least, I should have taken Lisa with me on a few practice drives. Instead, I assumed my fear would stay buried where it belonged."

She gave her head an angry shake. "Arrogance," she said. "Stupid, vainglorious arrogance."

She picked up her cup, tasted the tea, and made a face.

"I won't make that mistake again."

She put the cup down so hard tea slopped over the rim.

"Before we drive again," she looked at me hard "—and we *will* drive again—I'll take Lisa with me until we're both sure it's safe to have you in the cart."

Her smile was savage. "Then," she said, "I'll teach you to drive."

Chapter Forty-Two

Dear Sally,

You're not going to believe this. It's better than Ripley!

You know all those lessons I've been having on Firefly, and how much I've hated learning to ride? Remember Ethel? Mrs. Calhoun? She owns Cricket, only she calls him Promise.

I've been living in her house for a couple of weeks because my cough was keeping dear, delicate Jane awake.

Anyway, Ethel understands the one thing nobody here talks about: what it feels like to be afraid. If anybody else at this camp is scared of anything, they don't admit it. Especially if it's about horses. Maybe they think talking about it will scare them even more than they are already. Or more than they would be if they were ever scared. Which they're not.

You know what I mean.

Anyway, I've talked to Ethel about how riding scares me, so she took me for a carriage ride. Cricket is a driving horse. He doesn't like being ridden but he likes to drive.

My first time in a carriage was almost *too* exciting. Cricket headed back to the barn kind of fast and Ethel just froze. I had to help her get Cricket to slow down and stop.

Even though it wasn't perfect, I liked the feeling of being in the cart with Cricket out in front. I really liked being able to get him to stop. That was TOTALLY cool.

So when Ethel asked if I wanted to learn to drive, I couldn't wait.

It wasn't as easy as that, though. Ethel wanted to make a deal.

If I worked really hard at learning to ride—no more excuses, no more complaints—she would give me three driving lessons a week, plus lessons about the harness and hitching the horse to the cart.

She's going to do more than just teach me, though. She's decided to drive Cricket every day to make sure she won't have another freeze like she did today. If she's feeling scared, her granddaughter will sit in the cart with her, ready to take the lines if she has to.

I think she's making a mountain out of a mole-hill. I mean, nothing actually happened, did it? But, if that's what it takes, I'm all for it.

I can't wait for my first lesson. I'll let you know how it goes.

Love,
Charley

Chapter Forty-Three

I SPRINTED FROM THE CANOE dock to Ethel's house and arrived totally out of breath. She stood on her veranda holding a gift-wrapped package with a red bow on top. When I could breathe again, she handed it over.

The paper was blue, sprinkled all over with tiny red drawings of horses, whips, and carriages.

I carefully unstuck the tape and spread the paper out flat. A pair of brown leather gloves lay in a nest of tissue paper. I looked at Ethel with a question in my eyes.

"Driving gloves," she said.

Why, I wondered, did I need driving gloves?

"The leather of the glove adheres to the leather of the lines. Gloves help keep the lines from slipping through your fingers. If your horse is a puller—and Promise sometimes pulls—the gloves will protect your hands from blisters."

I gave a mental shrug. Cricket wouldn't pull

with me.

The gloves were as soft as butter. They fit perfectly.

Ethel picked up each hand and examined it.

"You don't want the gloves to be tight. Your hands, especially your fingers, need room to move. They need to be relaxed, just like when you ride."

I stroked one gloved hand with the other. I'd never felt anything so soft.

Ethel picked up the whip leaning against the wall. "This," she said, "is your leg."

Huh?

"When you sit on Firefly and want to tell him to do something, such as 'move over' or 'go faster,' what do you do?"

"You use your legs."

"Right. When you're sitting in the carriage and you want Promise to move over or go faster, how do you let him know?"

I get it! My legs would have to be pretty darn long.

Still, hitting him with a whip sounded like a terrible idea.

Ethel read my mind. She's good like that. "You don't hit him with it, except in an emergency. You *use* it, along with your voice and your weight and the way you sit, to give him directions. You'll get really good at dragging the lash over his haunches to make him speed up a little, and stroking his side with it to make him move away."

I must have looked especially blank, because Ethel continued.

"The whip is indispensable. You never drive without it. If you ever find yourself in a situation where you need him to go forward but all he wants to do is back up, you'll thank your lucky stars for the whip."

She looked down at the implement of torture with a fond smile on her face.

"This is one of mine from when I was learning. It's not pretty, but it's full of driving magic."

Magic? I had practical things to worry about.

"How do I hold the lines and the whip at the same time?" My hands are just as small as the rest of me.

She smiled. "It's a knack. It'll feel awkward for a bit, and then you'll get used to it." She stood up. "Got your helmet? Good. Let's go find Promise."

Cricket was standing in the aisle of the main barn. Carol was picking out his feet. I noticed how she had to pick up his hoof and hold it there. Whenever I did his feet he was a gentleman and picked them up for me.

His harness was hanging from its hook. It looked so much more complicated than a simple saddle and bridle, and I wondered if I'd ever learn how to harness him myself.

"Today you can just watch," Ethel said, in her teacher voice. "I want to get him hitched so you can get the feel of things. You can learn the harness later."

Ethel's hands flew and, in no time at all, he was enveloped in leather straps. She put a halter on over his bridle, clipped on a lead rope and handed it to me.

"Take him outside and line him up. I'll hitch him, and we can start."

I watched carefully as she attached him to the cart. Then she checked each fastening, touching it as she said its name out loud.

"It's easy to miss a connection," she said. "This way I can be sure everything's in place. Mistakes in hitching often end in tears—or worse."

The lines were coiled on the seat. She picked them up and climbed into the cart, then took the whip and motioned to me with her chin.

"Hop up quickly," she said. "You don't want to give him a chance to walk off or spook while you're getting in."

As soon as I was settled on the seat, she clucked softly and told him to walk.

We walked, and walked, and walked, and then we

walked some more. We wove through trees in the woods and stretched out along the long edges of the fields. When it looked like Cricket needed a break, we stopped in the shade of a spreading maple and relaxed.

Ethel had a basket stashed under the seat with a thermos and two plastic cups. Icy lemonade. Perfect for a hot afternoon.

"Well," she said. "Would you like to have a go?"

I was dying to try.

Ethel laid the lines in my gloved hands and showed me how to hold them.

"There are several different grips, but this is the simplest. Make a loose fist and lay the lines across the top of your index fingers. Trap them with your thumbs. If you want to let them out, just raise your thumbs the tiniest bit.

"You want to feel his mouth, just like when you ride, but you don't want to pull. Let him move your arms with his movement.

"Are you ready?" I nodded. "Then tell him what you want."

"Cricket," I said, my voice wobbling just a little, "walk up."

He flicked one ear back at me, as if to say, "Really? You mean it?" Then he lowered his head and started to walk.

It was heaven. I was mesmerized by the sway of his tail, the clip-clop of his hooves upon the track.

When I sit on Firefly, I can feel every twitch of his ears and quiver of his body. His feelings are part of me, and it's hard not to react.

Driving Cricket, sitting nine feet behind him, I was cushioned from all that. My connection with him was through two long strips of leather, stretching from the bit in his mouth to my hands.

What I felt through the lines was love.

We walked along the tracks through camp, passing campers and counselors without really seeing them. We were in our own private world, Cricket, Ethel and me.

Ethel didn't say much. She watched and listened to Cricket's footfalls, letting me sink into the drive like it was a warm bath. Instead of telling me where to go, she'd point, only commenting if I went off course.

Time passed as slow as pulled taffy and quicker than a wink. I was back at the barn in what seemed like seconds, watching Ethel back down off the cart and go to Cricket's head.

"Coil up the lines, Charley, and exit carefully. I'll see to it that Promise doesn't walk off."

I still had trouble getting out of the cart, but I managed without falling on my face. I went to Cricket's head and stroked his neck, and Ethel disconnected him from the cart. It was quite a process.

She led him out from between the shafts, and we went into the barn together. I watched as she took the harness off one piece at a time and hung the pieces on their hooks.

Cricket had sweat marks where the harness had been, and I scrubbed at them with a dandy brush. He leaned into the brush as if he liked it, so I kept on brushing. Then I checked his feet for stones. All clear.

"Take him in to the wash stall and rinse him off," Ethel said. "Then you can lead him outside for grass."

WE WANDERED AROUND OUTSIDE THE barn. Cricket had a look at the grass, but he was more interested in finding the perfect patch of dirt. When he levered himself down on his knees to roll, I didn't know what to do. Should I hang on to the rope or let it go?

I kept hold of the very end as he rolled on one side and then the other, grunting as he rolled. Hard work, but he seemed to like it.

"Brush off the dirt and take him home, Charley. He's probably ready for a nap. When he's settled, come back and we'll talk through the lesson."

I floated on air all the way to Cricket's paddock. I'd never been so happy in my entire life.

Chapter Forty-Four

Dear Sally,

I've started driving! My first lesson was yesterday, and man, is it complicated.

Take the harness. If you drop it on the ground, it looks like a pile of straps and buckles. When you look at each strap by itself, it makes absolutely no sense. Ethel just throws it on the horse and it all comes together, but I don't think I'll ever understand it.

Then there's hitching up. There's so much to get right. If you do it up wrong, the horse and the cart can come apart in really gruesome ways.

The reins are called lines and are they long! A whole pile of them sat in my lap while I was driving. They're buckled together at the end with a tiny loop you stick your pinky finger into. I'm not sure why. Maybe to keep them from getting tangled up?

And, finally, there's The Whip. Yeah, a real whip! The trouble is, with all those lines in my hands there's no room for the whip. And I have to carry it. No whip, no drive.

Ethel says I'll figure it out but, in the meantime, she holds the whip.

When Cricket was finally harnessed and hitched, and Ethel and I were both in the cart, she told Cricket to walk.

Sally, I've never felt anything like it. It was kind of like riding but totally different. I could feel every footfall, practically feel his breath, but there was this magical space between us. And even though I could feel every bump, every tussock of grass we ran over, it felt like we were floating.

I love sitting behind him and watching his butt sway. He lifted his tail and dropped manure, and I loved that, too. Did you know that when he poops, a horse's butt-hole looks like a rose opening?

When it was my turn, it took me about a year to get the lines arranged right, but once we started off I felt like we could go forever. All we did was walk, but who cares? Soon enough we'll be trotting.

Ethel was amazed at how willing Cricket was to walk. Usually he hates to walk, she says. He's a real "born to trot Morgan," just like in the book. Maybe he was looking out for me, but he never tried to speed up. He has a beautiful sprightly walk.

When I got out of the cart, I was so tired my knees buckled. Even Cricket was sweated up. Walking must be harder than it looks.

I love driving. Wish you'd been here to see.

Love,
Charley

P.S. Why haven't you written??? Are you still my best friend??

Chapter Forty-Five

WHEN I GOT TO THE kitchen, breakfast was waiting. French toast, crispy bacon—that was a first—and orange juice that tasted like it just left the tree. Frozen OJ never tastes this good.

Ethel had pulled out all the stops. Was she a) glad I was leaving? b) sorry to see me go but putting up a brave front? or c) worried that moving back to Cabin One was going to be a nightmare and wanting me to be well-fortified?

I'd stayed with her for two weeks. My cough was gone, my confidence was up, and I was aching to get back to cabin life. Well, maybe not aching. I knew I had to go back, but I wasn't looking forward to it.

Ethel came into the kitchen with a cup of herbal tea. I knew better than to turn it down. Her teas had certainly helped with the cough. What helped even more was sleeping in a room by myself, and not having to walk on eggshells in the cabin. I have no idea why Jane and Debbie and Pam don't like me, and not knowing keeps me on a knife-edge of anxiety.

I'd packed my bag last night. Now I just had to pick it up and walk out the door.

Ethel gave me a one-armed hug. "You'll be fine. And remember. We have a harness lesson before lunch. Don't be late."

The cabin was just where I'd left it. I walked up the stairs and opened the door.

Yellow Dog barreled past, almost knocking me down. She danced through the doorway and ran around the room, greeting everyone and wagging her tail so hard she almost couldn't walk. She stopped in front of Nancy, sat down, offered her paw, lay down, and rolled over. Then she lifted her head, gave Nancy a soulful look, and fell over dead.

Evie laughed so hard she had to sit down. Even Pam and Debbie cracked up. At least until Jane walked in with her we-are-not-amused Queen Victoria face. Then they wiped away their grins and tried to look severe.

"You're back," Jane said, in a sour voice. "Did you bring a note from the doctor, or are you still germ-infested and disgusting?"

I gave her the silent treatment and wished that, just once, she'd give it to me.

Yellow Dog ran to Jane, sat on her haunches, and

begged. Her tongue hung out of her mouth and saliva dripped on the floor. Jane turned on a heel and sat down on her cot. Yellow Dog ran over and sat up to beg some more.

Pam giggled. Debbie joined her, and pretty soon everyone was laughing. The dog dropped to the floor panting, and Jane walked out.

Yellow Dog looked affronted and followed Jane outside. She circled around till she was in front of her, sat down, and offered a paw. Jane turned away. Yellow Dog growled the tiniest growl and blocked Jane's path. She sat down and offered her paw again.

Jane looked at her very hard, then leaned over and shook the offered paw. She tried to keep walking, but Yellow Dog ran in front of her and collapsed on the path. When Jane stopped, the dog rolled over on her back and offered Jane her tummy to rub.

Nancy started to giggle and couldn't stop. Soon the rest of the cabin joined in.

Everyone crowded onto the porch to watch the drama. Jane made a move to leave, but the dog wiggled on her back until she blocked the path again, wagging her tail so hard her butt moved back and forth.

The laughter got louder, and finally Jane gave up and laughed too. She reached down and gave Yellow

Dog's tummy a pat. Then she walked back into Cabin One.

It struck me hard: I'd heard Jane sneer and snicker more times than I wanted to count. This was the first time I'd ever heard her laugh.

Chapter Forty-Six

ETHEL WAS WAITING FOR ME in the barn. After waiting another moment to let me catch my breath—I'd come by way of Cricket's paddock—she got started.

"Today we're going to learn the parts of the harness and what they do. The names are important, because you can use them to check your work before getting into the cart. If you say the names out loud, it's easier to see whether they're fastened correctly."

I'd never heard Ethel speak in such a strict, no-nonsense tone of voice. It was a little scary.

She pointed to a padded strap about five inches wide, with buckles on each end. "This is the breast collar, sometimes called the breastplate. The horse leans into it to pull the cart."

"Why is it called a collar? It looks more like a . . . well, like a bra."

Ethel made a face. "A little respect, please! This was the greatest technological advance of its age!"

Really? How great could a flat piece of leather be?

"A horse collar is basically a big padded donut that fits over the horse's head and rests on its chest. Leather straps or rope can be attached to each side of the collar and fastened to whatever needs pulling.

"Before collars existed, horses pulled with ropes around their necks. They couldn't pull anything heavy without crushing their windpipes. With the collar, they could use their chests to pull. It was an incredibly important step forward in the development of civilization."

I thought about rolling my eyes but decided against it. "So, why is this one flat?"

"Horses don't always pull heavy weights. This breastplate is part of a light harness, and a wide strap is all we need to use. Take it off the hook and bring it here."

Ethel ran the strap through her fingers thoughtfully. "What do you think connects to these buckles?"

I had no idea.

"Look through the harness and see if you can find anything that might fit."

The only things that looked at all likely were a couple of long straps about two inches wide. They had holes for a buckle at one end and a narrow slot about three inches long near the other. I pulled them off the hook and handed them to Ethel.

"Exactly! These are called traces. They connect the breastplate to the carriage. Without the traces, you can harness up all you want but the cart won't move an inch.

"The neck strap lies across the horse's neck and keeps the breastplate from slipping down. Hand me the saddle, would you?"

I remembered that from when I watched Ethel harness Cricket. It looked different today. A long strap was connected to the saddle with something funny at the end.

"This is the back strap. It goes from the saddle to the horse's quarters, connecting the front of the harness to the back."

I was drowning in detail but nodded to show I was listening.

Ethel held up the U-shaped piece of padded leather at the end of the back strap. "This is the crupper. Any idea what it does?"

I had an idea but shook my head. It couldn't be right.

"It goes under the horse's tail and keeps everything from sliding forward." She pantomimed holding up the tail and settling the crupper just where the tail comes out of the horse's rump.

Well, that was pretty gross. "What happens if the horse . . . uh . . . makes manure?" I asked, as delicately as I could. "Does the manure get stuck?"

Ethel smiled. "Of course not. And before you ask, no, the horse doesn't mind the crupper if it's in the right place."

The bugle for lunch echoed through the barn. Ethel patted my shoulder and gave me a little push toward the door. "Well, that hour went by fast. Go eat," she said. "I'll put this stuff away. We can finish the naming of parts tomorrow."

Chapter Forty-Seven

"WHEN THEY SAID WINDY PADDLE," I yelled, "they weren't kidding. At this rate we'll do the whole thing backwards."

The sky, blue when we got into the canoe, had gone gray, and fat clouds started to pile up over the mountains. Even as I wished for clearer skies, a low rumble of thunder rolled over the lake.

"Paddle faster, Birdie," I shouted. "We need to get back! I'll yell out the strokes so we can paddle together."

She turned halfway around to look at me.

"Don't look, just paddle!

"Stroke . . . stroke . . . stroke," I called. We moved a lot faster when we paddled at the same time.

We were doing the three-quarters-of-a-mile windy paddle canoe test, but I don't think Gloria meant this windy. We had just turned the second corner and were heading back to the dock when it suddenly got cold and fog rolled in over the lake.

"Stroke . . . stroke . . . stroke. . . ." I picked up the pace, hoping we could keep it up long enough to get back to shore.

The dock disappeared and the wind kept blowing.

"Slow down, Birdie," I called. "I can't tell which way to go."

"Charley, did you hear that?"

I stopped paddling. "Hear what?"

"It sounds like somebody yelling. The wind's so loud it's hard to tell." Birdy had to shout. "Listen for a second. Can you hear something?"

I listened, but all I heard was the wind and my own heartbeat. There was a flash and then, right away, a huge clap of thunder. I tried to see through the fog, but I was blind.

"There it is again," Birdie said. "Someone's yelling for help!"

Then I heard it too. A shrill voice shouting into the wind.

"Hey! You out there!" Birdie cried. "Keep yelling so we can find you!"

"Let's turn this boat around," I said. "Slowly. If they keep yelling, the sound should get louder when we face where it's coming from.

"Yell some more," I shouted. "Keep making noise."

The fog shredded in the wind and we could see a canoe. A girl in the bow was leaning over the side holding on to someone in the water. Birdie and I paddled as hard as we could, fighting waves thrown up by the wind. They hit us broadside and the canoe started to rock.

"Tell her to hold on to the gunwale," I shouted. "She could pull *you* in, too."

The two girls talked for a minute. Then the one in the water put one hand on the edge of the canoe and hung on. I could see she didn't want to let go of her partner's hand.

"Hold on to the boat with both hands," Birdie called. "It's safer."

We carefully paddled over to their canoe. The water was still rough, and we didn't want to lose control and hit them.

Allison was in the bow and Jane was in the water. Her paddle was heading to shore on its own.

"Jane, are you okay?" As soon as the words were out of my mouth, I felt stupid—but with most of her under water I couldn't tell. "Are you hurt?"

Her teeth were chattering. "Okay," she said. "Just cold."

"What happened?" Birdie asked.

Jane started to answer, but I cut her off. "Let's get you back in your canoe. We can talk after."

Easy to say, but I had no idea how to do it.

"If we can stabilize your canoe, you should be able to pull yourself up and get a leg in." Jane shook her head. She was shivering. "Just try it," I said.

We paddled around to the starboard side of Allie's canoe.

"Okay, Jane. Birdie and I will hold on to your canoe and Allie will pull you up. When she pulls, kick really hard. We'll hang onto your boat and lean way back to keep it from tipping over."

"Don't you understand anything? My wrist is hurt! I can't pull myself anywhere!"

I looked at her left arm. The elastic bandage she always wore was wrapped tight, and I could see bruises at both ends. Maybe she really couldn't pull.

"Try it with one arm," I said. "Give the biggest scissor kick you can, and then try to get your leg over the gunwale. Allie can pull you in the rest of the way."

"It won't work," Jane said. "I'll never get in like that! You don't know anything about it anyway."

"Just try. Otherwise you'll have to swim for it." Then I noticed she only had on her bathing suit. "Where's your life jacket?"

Jane looked furious and muttered something I couldn't hear.

"She took it off," Allie said. "The bottom of the boat was hurting her knees."

Jane scowled at me. "It's really stupid that there's no place to sit. I wanted something soft to kneel on."

There was nothing to say to that, so I didn't try.

Allie pulled the life vest from beneath a thwart and handed it down to Jane. She struggled to put it on in the water. It wasn't so easy to get the straps through the rings without someplace to stand, and Jane looked madder and madder. She finally gave up on the straps and just tied them in a knot.

"Ready? You'll kick and get your leg in the boat. Allie will pull you in. Birdie and I will keep your canoe from tipping. One, two three. Go!"

Jane kicked halfheartedly, Allie pulled on Jane's right arm, and Birdie and I hung on to their canoe.

We should have hung on to Allie. She landed in the water with a splash and came up coughing. Then she made a face and grabbed at her leg. It was bleeding right below her knee. She must've bashed it on the gunwale as she went in.

Jane screamed and kept on screaming. She thrashed around like a crazy person, and I was afraid she'd slide out of her life vest.

"What's wrong?" Birdie had to yell to be heard over Jane's screams. "Jane! What's the matter?"

"Blood in the water! It's going to get me!"

What was she talking about?

"Jane," Birdie said quietly. Jane had to stop screaming to hear her. "What's going to get you? You're not making sense."

"The monster! It lives in the lake and feeds on injured swimmers. It'll smell the blood and come to get me."

Jane sounded less crazy now that she wasn't screaming, but what she said made no sense at all. She'd stopped thrashing around and was climbing on top of Allie—who tried to fend her off with one hand while holding on to her shin with the other. Allie was having trouble keeping her head above water.

"Hey!" Birdie snapped. "Let go of Allie. You'll push her under."

Jane, still screaming, tried harder to get on top. Allie swallowed water and started to choke.

Birdie looked at me and slipped into the water. She put a hand under Jane's chin and pulled her away, hard, then grabbed her left arm and put it in a hammerlock. Jane struggled a little more and went limp.

Birdie looked at me and grinned.

"Two brothers who wrestle," she said. "I never thought it would come in handy."

She pulled Allie to our canoe and guided her hand to the edge. I looked for something to tie the cut up with—a bandana, a shirt, anything.

"Just hold on," I said. "We'll find something."

Jane sobbed, floating like a rag doll. Allie held on to her cut leg, looking worse by the minute, while Birdie helped her hold on to the canoe. We had one empty canoe and three people in the water. What were we going to do?

I couldn't think of a single thing. The fog was closing in again, and the temperature had dropped some more. I was starting to panic.

"Ahoy, campers! Hold tight."

Gloria was in a little skiff, its outboard motor putt-putting away. She cut the motor and glided over to us.

Sitting in the boat she just looked at us for a minute, trying to work out what had happened. Three girls were overboard, and one of them looked about to faint.

"Jane," Gloria said, in a no-nonsense voice. "Stop crying and swim over to the boat.

"Now hold onto my arms just above my wrists. Good. I'm going to back up and pull you in."

And, just like that, Jane was in the skiff, wrapped in a towel, still crying.

I turned back to Allie.

"She's cut her leg," I said. "We couldn't get her back in the canoe."

Gloria left Jane bundled up in the bow and turned to us. "You girls did well. You kept your heads, and everyone is safe. Birdie, help me get Allie into the boat, then we'll get you in, too. I'll come back later for the canoe."

I paddled back to the dock alone, trying to figure out what made Jane lose it. Blood in the water? Where did she get *that* from?

Just like in the movies, Gloria held a debriefing for Allie, Birdie and me. She wanted to know every little detail, from the time we heard voices in the fog until she showed up with the skiff. We went through it at least a hundred times before she frowned fiercely and said, "I guess we better learn how to get into a canoe from the water. Front and center tomorrow morning."

Then she smiled, and it was okay.

That night, after lights out, it came to me what the monster was all about.

The Creature from the Black Lagoon had come back to haunt us.

Chapter Forty-Eight

I WAS FUSSING WITH CRICKET'S mane. He was brushed, combed, and picked out, and I was ready to start braiding his tail when Ethel walked in. She hung his harness on the hook and checked him with a critical eye.

She picked up a back hoof. "Nice and clean," she said. "And all swept up, too."

I was jittering around, unable to stand still. Ethel had to repeat herself to get my attention.

"What's up with you today? Would you prefer to be doing something else? Harnessing a pony is an exacting job. If you make a mistake, you could pay a high price."

She was speaking in that too-precise way she has when her temper's fraying. I stopped shuffling my feet and tried to look attentive. I was interested. I couldn't wait to drive Cricket again. But the canoe adventure was bubbling inside me, struggling to get out.

"Sorry. I was thinking about something else."

I focused my eyes on the harness Ethel was starting to lay on Cricket's back.

"What do they call this?" she asked, pointing to the thing lying on the middle of his back. It was a funny shape and had a brass ring on either side. The girth was hanging down, and Ethel reached under him and buckled it up.

"Um, it's the saddle?"

"Is it or isn't it?"

I could feel myself turning red. "It is. It's the saddle, even though it doesn't look like one."

She pointed to a strap hanging from the saddle with a loop on the end.

"What's this for?"

I went totally blank.

Ethel waited for me to answer, then unbuckled the girth and hung the saddle back on the hook.

"Out with it, young lady. What's happened? You're jumping out of your skin and your mind is a million miles away."

She was right. All I could think about was the windy paddle and Jane.

Why couldn't she leave me alone? Everywhere I looked, Jane was there. In my face, in my way, in my life. I couldn't stand it.

"I had a strange kind of adventure. I can't stop thinking about it."

Ethel nodded for me to go on.

"It was a canoe test, and Birdie and I were out on the lake by ourselves. The weather got bad, and we were trying to paddle back. Jane and Allison had gone out ahead of us. We weren't supposed to even see them, but Jane had fallen out of her canoe and was in the lake."

"How did that happen?" Ethel asked. "It's not so easy to fall out of a canoe. Was she fooling around?"

"I don't know. She was holding on to Allison, and I was afraid Allison would fall in, too."

I could see the whole thing, like it was right in front of me, and it was getting me stirred up all over again.

"She wasn't even wearing her life jacket! How stupid is that? I tried to help her get back in the boat, but she didn't listen. She wouldn't even try. And, in the end, she did pull Allison out of the canoe.

"Then she got hysterical, and I thought Allison was going to drown. Jane was right on top of her, pushing her under the water."

Ethel looked at me for a second then looked away. "What happened then?"

I had to smile. "Birdie jumped in and put her in a

hammerlock to calm her down and keep her away from Allison. I loved it! Except now we had two canoes, three people in the water, and only me left to paddle back.

"Then Gloria showed up and took everybody back to the dock."

Ethel was quiet, maybe waiting for me to say something else. Finally she spoke.

"It sounds like it all turned out well, thanks to you and Birdie. Why are you upset?"

My eyes filled up and I rubbed them fiercely on my sleeve.

"She ruins everything! From the minute I got here, she's hated me. She was after me before I walked through the door, and half the camp agrees with her. It's bad enough I can't ride. I can't even make any friends. And now I have to help her? I should have let her drown!"

The words vibrated in the silence.

"Well, maybe not. But what can I do? I can't take it anymore."

"Hmm. No friends at all?"

I couldn't answer. Or, I knew the answer but couldn't say it. I listed friends at camp in my head: Nancy, Evie, Birdie, Allison. Ethel. And Carol. Even

Lois counted as a friend. Who else would put up with me? Not to mention Firefly, who had earned a place in my heart, the grumpy old thing. And, best of all, there was Cricket.

Ethel nodded as if she'd read my list. "And Jane," she said. "How many friends does she have?"

Only Pam and Debbie. And were they really friends? I didn't think so.

I shrugged.

"Is she a good rider?"

I shook my head. "She doesn't seem to like it. She can ride, but she's stiff in the saddle and always wears an ugly face."

More silence.

"The horses don't much like her, either. Maybe she smells funny or something, but they try to stay out of her way."

"So," said Ethel. "Who's got the better deal? You or Jane?"

I didn't want to answer. "Me, I guess."

"Does she strike you as a happy person?" Ethel asked.

I didn't want to discuss it or even think about it. Jane's happiness was not my problem.

But maybe her *unhappiness* was. Maybe that's why

she's so vicious. . . .

"I guess not. But why pick me to be her scapegoat? I've never done a thing to her." .

"Scapegoat. That's an interesting word to choose. Do you know what a scapegoat is?"

I shook my head.

"Does your family celebrate the Jewish holidays?"

"Sort of. At least we used to. Passover, anyway, and Chanukah, though Christmas is more fun."

"My first husband was Jewish. He was fascinated with Jewish history and religious law, so I learned more about it than I really wanted to know.

"On Yom Kippur, the Day of Atonement, the rabbi would take a goat—usually female, naturally—and recite all the sins of the community over the goat's head. Then the poor thing would be driven out of the village, taking all the sins with her. She was the scapegoat, taking away people's sins. It was supposed to make them feel better.

"Maybe Jane is trying to make herself feel better by making you feel terrible. What do you think?"

I shrugged again. "Maybe. But it doesn't work. I think it makes her feel even worse, so she gets meaner to me. I can't stand it anymore. How can I make her leave me alone?"

"That's a tough one. You've upped the ante by rescuing her. You were brave and resourceful, and your friends look up to you. Your adventure is probably the talk of the camp. I'll bet she's mad as stink right now."

I nodded glumly.

Ethel sat quietly for a long time. She finally sighed and said, "Any ideas?"

"Maybe . . ." I said slowly, ". . . I should get into her space, like sitting at her table at lunch or something. I could even follow her around, so everywhere she goes, I go too."

I giggled. "Maybe I could be like Mary's little lamb. Boy, would that make her crazy!"

Ethel nodded. "That's a pretty good idea. If it doesn't work, you might try something else."

"Like what?"

"You might try to be her friend."

Chapter Forty-Nine

Dear Sally,

Some people never get it right, and Jane is wrong squared. Or maybe cubed. Every word out of her mouth is a knife.

She knows nothing about carriage driving, but she gave me a lecture about rubbish horses who drive because they're too dumb to do anything else. Then she said I like driving because I'm too chicken to ride!

This from the girl who was scared witless to get back on Jack and used her sore wrist to skip lessons.

I stomped off to see Cricket, smoke billowing out of my ears. I was so upset I forgot to watch where he was putting his feet. My baby toe is now Technicolor purple and it's hard to put my boot on.

Ethel is always reminding me to keep calm around horses, and now I know why. I'm afraid to tell her about my toe.

Have you ever been stepped on? I really hope you're smarter around horses than I am.

Please write and tell me.

Love,
Charley

Chapter Fifty

I STARTED THE GAME ON the way to lunch. Instead of walking with Birdie and Allison, I rushed up to Jane and accidentally bumped her off the trail.

"Oh, sorry!" I said, dripping honey. "Are you okay? Did I knock your poor arm? It must still hurt an awful lot, huh?"

Birdie walked past but didn't say anything. She didn't have to. Her body language said it all.

"What have you been doing?" I asked sweetly. "Stepped on any good wasps lately?"

Jane looked daggers at me. She'd turned dead white, then bright red. I hoped she wasn't going to have a heart attack and blame me. I might end up in jail.

"I wonder what's for lunch today. I'm hoping for hamburgers. What do you think?"

A wordless growl from Jane set me off. I had to choke down my giggles, and pretty soon I was choking for real. Maybe I'd be the one with the heart attack.

Evie was the next one to pass by. Always polite, she

said "Hi, Charley, hi, uh, Jane?" then scuttled away before Jane could skewer her. I started to laugh and choke all over again.

Jane ignored me. She walked faster, but I stuck with her, and pretty soon we had caught up to Pam and Debbie. Jane started to puff up, sure that I wouldn't stick around if it was three against one. She made a horrible face, but I paid no attention.

I jabbered on about canoeing, and swimming, and letters from Dad (that I didn't read). Pam and Debbie looked confused. Jane said nothing. When we got to lunch I followed them in and sat at their table. I had to nudge Jane out of the way to make room to sit down.

I ate as fast as I could at our totally silent table, then left for a visit with Cricket before free swim. I French-braided his mane and told him all about my plan to drive Jane crazy. He didn't have much to say, especially when he realized there weren't any carrots in my pocket.

Before I could use a rubber band on the final section, he shook his head and it all came undone.

I ran to the waterfront and arrived just in time to ask Jane to be my buddy. She turned her back and pretended I wasn't there, so I buddied up with Evie instead. We had a competition to see who could stay underwater the longest. Evie can dive deeper, and stay on the bottom longer, than anyone I've ever met.

Every chance I got I stared at Jane until she had to look back. Then I'd quickly look the other way. It was more fun than I'd had in weeks.

Chapter Fifty-One

IT WAS HARD TO SIT still. Lunch was over, and my parents weren't here yet. I was supposed to stay in the cabin to meet them, but I'd waited long enough. They weren't coming, and it was my own fault.

The camp was full to bursting with parents. There was an afternoon program that would end with a fancy supper, and camper songs and skits afterward. I had a part in the songs, but the skits were put together by drama students. All I'd have to do is watch and clap like mad.

Evie and I were the only ones left in Cabin One. I was about to ask her to come on a Little Lamb foray when her parents popped their heads through the door. She ran over to hug them, looking relieved. New Jersey is far away, and Evie's a worrier.

So that left me.

A small reconnaissance was in order. Where was Jane, and what was she doing? I was determined to find out.

I drifted over to the arts and crafts hut. I hate even being in the room, but it was always a good place to find Jane. It takes all kinds, as my father likes to say.

The hut was crowded. Campers' best creations hung on the walls and covered the craft tables. None of mine were on display. I hadn't made a thing. A project to teach me French braiding? Now *that* would have been useful, but the closest I could find was the spiral technique of making lanyards.

If you weren't a gym teacher, why would you need a lanyard?

Girls were pointing out their projects to admiring parents. Everyone was talking at once, and the noise was overwhelming. Jane wasn't there.

I tried the waterfront next. A big free swim was happening, but nope, no Jane.

I went back to the cabin to think about strategy. Wandering around at random wasn't going to work. The weekly schedule was no help. Because of Parents' Weekend, everything was different.

Where would Jane take her parents? What would they want to see?

Horses. This is a horse camp. Maybe Jane's parents would want to see the horses.

I headed for the barn.

An intermediate class was underway in the ring, and there was Jane, leaning on the rail, clenching her teeth. I could see a little muscle in her jaw jumping.

Her parents looked tenser than she did, if that was even possible. Her mother examined the riders with a lemon-sucking face, and her father looked like he'd rather be anywhere else.

It was obvious where Jane got her attitude. I felt a sneaking sense of pity. My parents might be messed up, but *hers*. . . .

Pity was not what I needed to feel when playing Mary Had a Little Lamb.

I sauntered over to the rail and smiled. "Hey, Jane, how's it going?"

I expected a reaction, but what I got from Jane was relief flavored with desperation. She was glad to see me!

"Hi, Charley. We're just, uh, watching the lesson. Pretty good, isn't it? I think they'll start the jumping soon."

She clearly needed help and, just my luck, there was no one suitable in sight. I couldn't just walk away. I turned to the parents and took a deep breath.

"You must be Mr. and Mrs. Blake. I'm Charley Rittenberg. I'm with Jane in Cabin One."

I stuck out my hand. After an awkward silence, her

dad reached over to shake it. It was a hot day, but his hand was icy cold.

"Nice to meet you," he said. "It's always good to meet a friend of Jane's."

I glanced at Jane. She looked back out of panicky eyes.

"We're in Beginners together," I said. Jane closed her eyes. What was going on here?

"Beginners?" asked Mrs. Blake. "Jane's no beginner. She's been riding for years. In the fall she'll start the show circuit with her new pony."

Jane looked sick.

"Is Lois still the head riding coach?" her mother asked. "I need to have a word with her."

No one said a thing.

"Immediately!"

Jane looked like she wanted to crawl under the nearest boulder and die. I'd have helped if I could, but I had no idea what to do. In the end, I just stood next to her, shoulder to shoulder, like in the song.

With her teased-up hair and hatchet of a nose, Mrs. Blake had the look of a huge bird of prey. She stomped into the barn like an avenging eagle.

Lois was in her office with a girl from Cabin Four and her parents, looking at something in a notebook.

When she saw the invasion of the Blakes, she sighed, closed the notebook and looked apologetically at her visitors. They sized up the situation and left without looking back.

Lois sat up straight, exhaled, and smiled. "So happy you could come, Mrs. Blake. Jane is certainly making progress this year. I'm sure you'll want to see her ride."

"That is precisely why I'm here. Why was Jane placed in the beginners class *again*, and why on earth was I not informed?"

Lois looked up. "Why don't you girls go visit Promise. I'm sure Charley will be happy to introduce you."

We couldn't get out of there fast enough.

Jane was *not* going to meet Cricket. I'd been nice to her for a few awkward minutes, but that didn't make me her best friend. We weren't any kind of friends and weren't likely to be.

"Bye, see ya," I said as I peeled off, running towards Cricket's paddock. "Good luck with the riding."

Jane flinched, and for a whole second I felt bad about leaving her alone.

Then I felt fine and kept on running.

Chapter Fifty-Two

JANE DIDN'T TAKE "BYE" FOR an answer. The footsteps behind me got louder and louder, and pretty soon she was running next to me.

I was too busy running myself to say anything to chase her away, but I kept turning my head to give the dirtiest looks I could manufacture.

She ignored me and kept on running.

I needed to get rid of her so I could visit Cricket for our afternoon heart-to-heart. Lois should never have invited Jane to meet him. He was mine, not something else for Jane to ruin!

I slowed down to catch my breath. The cough was gone, but some of its effects lingered on, especially when I was stressed. I couldn't run forever like I used to.

As soon as I slowed down, Jane barreled past. She didn't exactly force me off the path, but getting out of her way seemed like a smart idea. I waited for her to slow down, too, but she speeded up and left me behind.

I stopped running and looked for a way through the little woods to Cricket's field. The trees were thick and the undergrowth was tough and tangled. I forced my way, picking up a few scratches on my legs and arms. With a little luck, I'd be totally out of sight before Jane realized I wasn't there.

When I finally broke out of the trees, I was near enough to Cricket to kiss his face. He must have heard me thrashing around and come to the fence to see who was having fun without him. Jane was nowhere to be seen.

That was the good news.

The bad news? Carol was sitting on the fence waiting for me.

I stopped in front of her, out of breath. What could she want?

"Hi, Charley," she said. "Fancy meeting you here."

Ha, ha! This is where I was most afternoons during arts and crafts. As if Carol didn't know. If I pretended she wasn't here, maybe she'd go away.

"I've just come from the office. A visitor is waiting to see you."

A visitor? Why not "your parents"? Maybe it's not Mom and Dad. Maybe they were in an accident. They had a fight while driving up to camp and crashed the car. It's the sheriff who's waiting for me in the office. My heart was a fist clenched in my chest. It made me dizzy.

"Take it easy, Charley." Carol had an arm around me, holding me up. "Let's walk back and see what's happening."

Dad's shabby blue Nash Rambler was parked under a tree near the office.

Does that mean Mom didn't come? If they came together it would be her car. Mom hates being a passenger and refuses to drive Dad's car.

My feet were stuck to the ground.

The door opened, and Dad ran down the stairs. He pulled me into an enormous hug but didn't say a word. He just breathed heavily into my hair.

"Where's Mom?" I croaked. "Is she inside?"

Dad gave me a last squeeze and stepped away. He looked at me with such a sad expression, I started to cry.

I turned around so he couldn't see my face.

"She didn't come, did she." It wasn't a question.

Dad put his hands on my shoulders and gently turned me towards him. "I know you're having a hard time with the separation, but it's a fact. We all have to learn to live with it. Let's go for a walk, and you can show me around."

I spun away from him and ran. I never wanted to see him again.

Chapter Fifty-Three

I FELT LIKE A RABBIT with dogs hot on its trail. I needed a place to hide where Dad—or Carol, or Ethel—wouldn't think to look.

Cricket's paddock was out of bounds. It's the first place they'd go. The woods are too small for hiding. They'd find me in no time.

I ran past our cabin, checking out the space under the deck. Too tight.

Wait a sec. Cabin Three has a high deck with bushes near the front. I could squeeze in behind them and disappear.

Parents sat chatting on the deck. No way could I slide underneath and hide behind the bushes.

There was only one other place where no one would look.

Arts and Crafts.

Brilliant! No one who knew me even a little would look for me in the arts and crafts hut. I wouldn't be in the hut, anyway. I'd be underneath.

It was going to be tricky. The place was crawling with kids and parents. If I walked in like I belonged, no one would believe it. I was known around camp as the anti-A&C camper. It was a little like publicly not believing in God.

The best way to play it was in their faces. I walked right in and made a big deal of looking around.

"Has anybody seen my dad?" I asked.

No one answered, so I said it again, trying to look peeved.

Blank looks. No one cared. Perfect.

I sat on a bench at the back of the room and pretended to be interested in the projects on display. I looked around to check who was there, then dropped a potholder over the edge.

Muttering something about butterfingers, I left the room.

The arts and crafts hut is built on a hill, and there's lots of space between the floor and the ground on the far side. I crawled in and heaved a huge sigh of relief.

It was cool and damp under the hut. Years of fallen leaves were quietly rotting away. The smell made me want to sneeze. I grabbed my nose and squeezed hard enough to make my eyes water.

I heard a sniffle. Then a sob. I peered through the

gloom. Jane sat about five feet away with her head on her knees.

I felt like I'd been kicked in the stomach. Was there no place I could go that Jane wouldn't follow me?

"Stop following me!" She hissed. "No matter where I go, you're there too. What do I have to do to make you leave me alone?"

I stammered something incoherent. Tears were sliding down Jane's face and soaking her T-shirt. She looked miserable. I told myself I didn't care. Jane could cry all she wanted. It had nothing to do with me.

I could think it, but I couldn't feel it. I was miserable enough myself.

"What are you doing here?" I whispered. "Aren't you supposed to be in a lesson?"

She gave me her world champion are-you-even-stupider-than-I-thought look, then put her face back on her knees and sobbed some more.

"Hush up! Someone will hear you. *You* might want to be found, but I certainly don't! What's the matter with you, anyway?"

Jane looked up with her nasty face on. "Like you could care! It's none of your business, so butt out!"

"I can't butt out. I don't want my father to see me. So calm down and shut up!"

She stopped crying. "Why are you hiding from your father?"

"Why are you under the hut?"

Jane looked down and started rolling the hem of her T-shirt between her fingers. She was quiet for the longest time, just rolling and unrolling her shirt, staring at the ground. My nose started to itch again, and I pinched it closed.

"You saw my mother. She's a witch. Wouldn't you hide?"

I would, actually, but it didn't seem polite to say so.

"What was she so mad about?"

"She's always mad at someone, but she's maddest at me. I came to camp this summer with an assignment. I had to ride well enough to look good on the pony they're buying for me to show."

"But. . . ."

"Yeah. I know," Jane said, in a flat tone of voice. "I'm a lousy rider. So I lied. I wrote saying I was moved up to the intermediate class, then made up a bunch of stuff about how well I was doing."

She looked over at me and started to cry again. "It was stupid. I knew Parents' Weekend was coming and I'd get caught, but I couldn't help it. I wrote this whole story about camp, and riding, and how much fun I was having."

I waited to see what came next.

"And all the time I was just so angry! I don't belong here. I don't like riding. I can't stand horses. I want to be home doing what I like to do."

"If you don't like horses, why are you at riding camp?"

"That's the Sixty-Four Thousand Dollar Question. My mother likes horses. She was a big shot in the show circuit when she was a teenager and wants us to do it again—for her. My sister's okay. She's pretty and tall and looks great on a horse. She's a natural, just like my mother. They can't understand that I don't want to ride."

"If you don't like horses, what *do* you like?"

Jane looked away and took a minute to answer.

"I like bikes," she said shyly. "I like going really fast on bikes."

Wow. I sure hadn't expected that.

"Bikes aren't like horses. They don't get scared and do dumb things. Like Jack. If you make a mistake, maybe you fall off, but it's not because the bike tried to buck you off or anything. It's just you, the bike, and physics."

"Physics?" This conversation was getting weirder by the minute.

"Yeah. Riding a bike is all about physics."

Chapter Fifty-Four

I STILL NEEDED A SAFE place to hide from Dad. The cabin? I wanted a little human contact, but not that badly. Cricket? No. Firefly? Nobody'd look for me there, but he probably wouldn't let me in his stall without carrots. . . .

I walked to the barn anyway, hoping for inspiration.

I stuck my head around the door and pulled it right back. A group of seniors sat on the floor cleaning bridles and gossiping.

The door to the Boarders' Barn was open a crack and I slid inside. It was dark and cool, and the only sound was the quiet chomping of hay. I looked down the aisle, hoping for a place to hide, but I didn't know any of the horses. So which stall was safe?

An enormous brown muzzle poked itself over a stall door. I heard a soft questioning whicker and went to say hello. The muzzle was connected to a long bay face with what looked like white lightning running down it.

The Brontosaurus! Lois's Thunderbolt. The name

floated into my brain like magic.

He whickered again and bobbed his head up and down. Either he was hungry—and the wisp of hay hanging out of his mouth made that unlikely—or he was lonely. It reminded me of when I met Cricket, and my heart gave a joyful thump.

I opened the top half of his stall door and leaned in. He brought his face down to mine and we exchanged breaths. It made me feel recognized. Acknowledged. Something. Whatever it was, it made me feel happy and safe.

I opened his door a few inches and sidled in, closing the top half to be less visible to anyone walking by. We stood together for a few quiet minutes, his head on my shoulder and my arm around his neck. I had to stand on tiptoe, and he had to practically bend his knees, but it worked.

The day caught up with me all at once. My knees buckled, and I slid down the wall to the floor and closed my eyes.

Chapter Fifty-Five

STILL GROGGY WITH SLEEP, I heard Ethel ask a question.

Dad's voice answering her woke me up fast. What was he doing in the Boarders' Barn? Why was he talking to Ethel?

I sat up, leaned against the wall and listened. Sounded like she was showing him Cricket's carriage.

"My granddaughter Lisa loves this old carriage. Really more a cart than a carriage, actually, a kind of runabout. Drive it to the store or maybe drop a child off at school. Not fancy. Just two wheels and a coat of paint. I bought it during the war to save on gasoline."

What was she going on about? Dad knew nothing about horses, and now he had to learn about carriages? I don't think so!

"Promise—the horse Charley calls Cricket—was happy pulling a cart. That was lucky for him, because he flatly refused to be a riding horse. He'd stand stock still and, if you pushed him forward, like as not he'd lie down with you and try to roll.

"Lisa hauled this old thing out of a shed last winter, tightened all the screws and stripped the paint. Then she painted it Austin Healey green and tarted up the fittings. I assure you, the gold racing stripes are neither original nor appropriate."

Dad broke into Ethel's monologue with the voice he uses when he's trying to sound reasonable.

"What do carriages have to do with anything? Charley came here to learn to ride, and her counselor—Carol?—says she's had a really hard time. It's not like her to be afraid, so what's going on?"

I cracked the top door of Thunderbolt's stall so I could watch. Dad and Ethel were standing near the carriage, and Dad seemed to be examining the paint job.

"Let's back up a bit, Mr. Rittenberg," Ethel said, leaning on her cane. "When we accepted Charley as a last-minute camper, we took a punt. She's the first girl to come here with no riding experience whatsoever. We hoped that, by getting her started with horses correctly right from the beginning, we could avoid some of the problems that develop when children learn to ride without sufficient instruction."

Dad started fidgeting and glanced around the barn.

He was looking for an escape route.

Ethel was oblivious. She cleared her throat and he brought his gaze back to her face.

"Our grand experiment didn't work out exactly as planned. Firefly, Charley's horse for the summer, is very different from the horses she knew from books. He's an old campaigner, nearly thirty, and doesn't bond quickly with new riders.

"He's a great caretaker, which is why we gave Charley to him. But at first, anyway, he's anything but touchy-feely. Charley found that lack of emotional connection terrifying. Learning to ride was not the joy she expected. It was more like a glass mountain she had to climb, with shards everywhere."

Dad stood with his head down and listened.

"Her first lesson was a disaster."

Dad's head came up.

"Not only was she afraid—which she had not expected—she didn't even manage to get on her horse. She left the lesson in tears, ran past her cabin into the woods, and ended up in a secluded paddock far away from barns and arenas and snarky sarcastic cabin mates.

"Promise—Cricket—was in that paddock. He trotted up to the fence and demanded she become his friend."

Ethel smiled and shook her head.

"Charley fell in love." She smiled again. "The feeling was mutual."

"That's all well and good," Dad snapped, "but it doesn't answer my question. What's with the carriage? What does it have to do with her fear? How does it help?"

He was practically stuttering.

"Riding really scared Charley. Firefly wasn't the friend she expected him to be. The girls in her cabin gave her a hard time, and she had nowhere to turn."

"Exactly! So what did you do to help her? She's only eleven! Her parents have separated, her world is crumbling, and you come up with a cute little green carriage? How is that the answer to anything?"

Ethel propped her cane against one of the carriage shafts.

"When she met Promise, her world came back into focus."

She was quiet for a minute.

"If he were an educated saddle horse, we could have made Promise Charley's summer horse. She would have felt safe with him. That wasn't possible. We had to come up with a different plan.

"Charley has spent a lot of time with me this summer, and I've come to know her well. I introduced her to carriage driving as a reward for all the hard work she's put into learning to ride—and also as a way for her to work with Promise. Maybe she can't ride him, but she can certainly learn to drive him."

Ethel laughed a little. "It turns out she's a natural. Connected, calm and fearless. It's as if driving a horse is what she was born to do. Assuming, of course, that the horse is Promise."

Dad shoved a fist into a pants pocket. He was clenching and unclenching so hard it looked like a mouse was trying to escape.

"Her first carriage ride did not go according to plan. Promise sped up on his way back to the barn. I froze, deep in a flashback of a carriage-driving accident I had many years ago. Charley helped slow him down and got us home safely. It was remarkably cool-headed behavior for someone who had never even sat in a carriage before."

Ethel looked up with an embarrassed smile. "Sorry. I didn't expect to go on like that."

Dad didn't smile back. His face was red, shoulders up around his ears. He looked ready to explode.

"Tell me about the accident," he said, so quietly it was almost a whisper.

I knew that voice. It was a very bad sign.

Ethel crossed the aisle and picked up her cane. She ran her hands back and forth along the curved grip. "There's no need to go into the details," she said.

Dad's shoulders moved higher.

"There's every need," he said, his voice still just above a whisper. "This is my daughter's life we're talking about! If you can have an accident—you, who's been driving all your life—how is Charley going to manage?"

By the time he finished he wasn't whispering any more.

Ethel sighed and looked away. "Accidents are almost always the result of human error. When you take error out of the equation, what's left is gore. Not really interesting when all is said and done."

"Trust me," Dad said. "I'm interested.

Ethel shrugged. She didn't look happy.

"It was a bad day, from start to finish. I had a fight with my husband at breakfast. Then I hitched my horse and took him for a drive when I had no business even setting foot inside the barn. I knew better. That's the thing. I knew better and did it anyway."

She walked the aisle restlessly.

"Temper has no place around horses. They're sensitive, and they pick up the energy. A safe horsewoman has her adrenaline under control, and mine wasn't. I drove to the woods and started playing tag with the trees, driving in and out between them as fast as I could go.

"It was fun. It calmed me down.

"Then I made a rookie mistake. 'Just one more time,' I thought. 'I'll make it the fastest run yet.' Of course, it wasn't. The carriage clipped a tree and swerved. I over-corrected and clipped another tree. The carriage flipped.

"Luck was with me. I could have been in a wheelchair for the rest of my life, but I broke my pelvis, not my neck. After three months in bed, I got up and walked away. My horse wasn't so lucky."

She stopped pacing and stared at the floor, breathing fast.

"You have got to be kidding!" Now Dad was practically shouting. "You're nearly killed or paralyzed in a driving accident, and you want to teach my daughter to drive? Are you crazy?"

He walked over to the carriage, too agitated to stand still, and plucked the whip out of its holder. It was four-and-a-half feet long with two feet of lash on the end and very springy. He studied it for a moment, then turned the whip around and held it about a foot down from the handle. He smacked the handle against his palm as he talked.

"What was this 'flashback'?" *Smack.* "What would have happened if Charley hadn't stepped in?" *Smack.* "Another crash?" *Smack.*

"A broken neck this time?"

He took a long, shaky breath and put the whip back where it belonged. He'd calmed down, and that scared me more than his shouting did.

Chapter Fifty-Six

"WELL," DAD SAID FLATLY. "THAT'S the end of driving for Charley. It's too dangerous. Riding's bad enough, and she doesn't even like it. I want her to come home in one piece. Tomorrow."

I slammed Thunderbolt's stall door open. The top half swinging wildly back and forth sounded like cherry bombs exploding.

I charged into the aisle and stuck my face as close to Dad's as I could reach.

"No!" I yelled. "You've got it all wrong! Cricket is the only good thing that's happened since I got to this horrible place. He's my friend. He looks after me. He would never do anything to hurt me!"

Dad stepped back, wiping my spit off his face with one hand.

"Charley," he said calmly. "You don't understand. This whole riding camp thing has been a mistake from the get-go. It's time to call it a day and come home."

His hands were shaking and he shoved them back

into his pockets.

So much for being calm, I thought. That'll teach him.

"No, you're the one who doesn't understand! You and Mom made me come here. You knew I didn't want to leave home, so you bribed me with a camp that had horses. 'Come Meet Your Summer Horse!' the brochure said. Who could resist that?

"So I came. It wasn't what I expected, and riding scared me half to death. Cricket has been the only thing that keeps me going. Ethel's teaching me to drive, and I love it.

"Is it dangerous? Of course it's dangerous! Riding a bike is dangerous! Crossing the street is dangerous! You can stay in bed your whole life, then get up in the night to pee, fall down the stairs, and break your neck!"

Dad reached out and touched my shoulder. I shook his hand off and backed away. I tried to speak more calmly myself.

"I love Cricket and I love driving. I won't give them up."

Thunderbolt leaned over the door to his stall and blew down the back of my neck. He hardened my resolve.

This was one battle I wasn't going to lose.

Chapter Fifty-Seven

DAD'S ANSWER WAS STONY SILENCE. Ethel was silent, too. Were we going to stand like this till the next Ice Age?

Then Yellow Dog ran into the barn and skidded to a stop in front of Dad. When he ignored her, she jumped up and pawed at his chest.

"Get off me!" he snarled, pushing her away.

"Come here this instant!" I hissed. Yellow Dog left Dad and sat in front of me. She was quivering with hurt feelings. "Never mind," I whispered. "He didn't mean it."

Ethel moved forward and dusted off her hands, putting my outburst and the argument with Dad behind her.

"Well, well," she said, looking directly at me. "You've been pretty hard to find today, but I'm glad you're with us now. I thought you might like to introduce your dad to Promise and maybe show him around the camp a little."

"Cricket," I mumbled.

It was a little game we played. She wouldn't call him Cricket, and I never called him Promise.

"Why not bring him over here to us? We'll wait in the shade while you run around. Age has to have some privileges."

I looked at her carefully, wondering what she was up to. She'd never asked me to do anything like this before—and she *never* talks about how old she is.

"His halter should be hanging on the fence. Stop at the barn to pick up a stick. He has to mind his manners when you lead him."

Whatever. I shrugged and headed off. It was hot and sticky, but I was always glad of an excuse to see my boy. No matter how bad I was feeling, Cricket made things better just by being there.

Yellow Dog danced around me all the way to the barn. I grabbed a riding crop and headed to Cricket's paddock, trying hard to calm down. My aching foot reminded me what can happen when you're all hyped up around a horse.

Ethel's always telling me that most horse accidents happen on the ground. I knew the lecture by heart: "You think a broken foot is trivial, young lady? Just wait until a horse treads too close behind and steps on your heel. He needs to walk next to you, at your shoulder. Use the crop to keep him from bulling ahead."

Cricket had just woken up from his afternoon nap. His mane and forelock were full of twigs and dead leaves, and his shoulder was dusty from rolling. He shook himself and wandered over to say hello and check my pockets for treats. I love it when he sniffs me all over, just in case something delicious is hidden in a new place.

I looped the lead rope over his neck and slipped on his halter. Then I used a Pony Club knot to tie him to the fence.

It was another of Ethel's rules: "Always secure the lead rope. Don't assume he's going to stay put. If something scares him and he runs, the lead could trip him up. He could be seriously hurt, maybe even break a leg."

That was not something I wanted to think about.

With Dad and Ethel waiting, there was no time for a full-on grooming session. I gently cleared the landscape from his long wavy mane, curried up the dirt and dust and brushed it away. I had to smile, remembering how daunting I'd found grooming Firefly to be. I thought I'd never learn how to manage the brushes, let alone check his feet for stones.

I ran a brush through his mane and tail, kissed him on the nose, and pulled on the end of the rope. The quick-release knot untied itself. I gathered up the lead, took my position, and said "Cricket, walk up!"

Cricket is a pushy little horse, always wanting to be the leader. His position of choice is with his head about two feet in front of me and just about treading on the edge of my right foot.

If—when—he snuck ahead of me, I was supposed to use the crop to remind him of his proper place. A tap on his chest usually put him back where he belonged, but sometimes a smack was in order. If I really focused, I could stop the encroachments before they got started with a sharp grunt that meant "Back off you rotten scallywag." But mostly I missed his careful forward sneak.

When he moved too close to me, an elbow in the ribs could be effective, along with a mean-sounding "Over!"

Walking safely with Cricket means eternal vigilance, and I'm horribly distractable. When we're together my mind loses itself in daydreams of the fun we're going to have, and I kind of drift away from the job at hand.

Ethel's working hard to correct my thinking.

When we got near the Boarders' Barn, Cricket put on the brakes. Yellow Dog wanted to keep moving. She ran circles around us, leaping in the air every few feet to push Cricket on. He ignored her, and I—well, I tried to ignore her, too. I even threatened her with the riding crop, for all the good that did.

DAD AND ETHEL WERE WAITING under the cluster of apple trees outside the barn. Ethel sat on a decrepit old bench, and Dad stood a few feet away staring at what looked like nothing. He was eating an apple.

I could see Cricket's nose working, trying to figure out who the stranger was and what he was holding that smelled so good.

Ethel gestured towards the half-eaten apple.

"Hold it out flat on your palm," she said to Dad. "Keep your fingers together and your thumb close to your hand. Stretch your arm out in front of you."

Cricket looked interested. Dad looked nervous.

Ethel nodded to me and I made a clicking noise with my tongue. Cricket and I took a few steps forward, and he stretched out his neck to see what Dad had. One more step and Cricket was close enough to grab. Instead, he sniffed Dad's hand then gently lipped the apple into his mouth.

The crunch of his teeth was as loud as a landslide.

Dad exhaled and moved back a step. I could see beads of sweat on his upper lip. Could he really have been that scared?

I reran the film of my first lesson with Firefly. Maybe it's genetic.

I could feel Cricket thinking about moving in for another treat. I growled at him—just a tiny growl, but I meant it. He stayed where he was. I scratched his neck and whispered "Good boy!" He gave me a what-did-you-expect look and sighed.

"Well," Ethel said, in her school-teacher voice. "That was nicely done."

She glanced at Dad, then shook her head slightly.

"I can see you're more impressed that Promise didn't bite off your fingers than at how neatly Charley managed that encounter."

Dad looked blank.

She smiled at me. "It may have looked to you that Charley was taking the pony for a casual walk. No big deal, nothing to worry about.

"Charley monitored every step of that walk. She made sure Promise stayed where he belonged so he couldn't knock into her or step on her foot. She kept his attention on her and made sure he minded his manners.

"She did an excellent job, and so did he. But if her mind had been in the clouds, or just worrying about what you were doing here talking to me, the outcome might have been very different.

"You should be proud."

She turned to me. Uh oh, I thought. What now?

"Why don't you leave Promise here with me and take your father to meet Firefly. He's heard a lot about him and must be anxious to see him in the flesh."

She dug into her pocket and brought out a few wilt-ed-looking carrots. Cricket immediately perked up.

"Take these to sweeten the pot."

Dad didn't look too keen, but with Ethel's eyes drilling holes in his chest, what choice did he have?

We walked in uncomfortable silence. Yellow Dog slipped away to hang out with Cricket, and then it was just my dad and me with nothing to say.

Chapter Fifty-Eight

IT WAS GETTING DARK WHEN we arrived at the barn. Time had flown by, and supper was long over. I didn't think Firefly would be all that thrilled to have visitors this late, but the carrots would probably win him over.

I thought of him slobbering orange drool all over my shirt on the first day of camp and had to smile.

The barn was buzzing. Five or six girls clogged the aisle, and Lois, in the tack room, was on the phone. A funny time to be calling someone, I thought. Allison was leaning against the wall.

"What's going on?" I asked.

"Firefly's not in his stall," she replied. "When Lois came to do barn check, the stall door was open and Firefly was gone. Nobody's seen him since his evening feed."

A cold chill stole down my back, and goose pimples popped up on my arms. Firefly gone? I shivered.

"This is my dad," I said. "I brought him around to meet my summer horse. Dad, this is my friend Allison.

We canoe together."

Dad nodded awkwardly.

"How do you do?" Allison asked politely. She didn't wait for an answer, but turned towards Lois as she left the tack room.

"I've called around," Lois said. "Nobody's seen him. He was off his feed this evening, which isn't like him, but otherwise he seemed fine. I have no idea how he got out of the stall or why he would even want to. Firefly loves his routine. He's not a wanderer—not like some horses I could name."

A girl I didn't know giggled. If there was a joke, I didn't get it.

"Everybody grab a buddy and come with me," Lois said. "We'll split up and look."

Dad was embarrassed. "Do you want me to stay? I can go with you while you look for your horse."

"That's okay, Dad," I said. "We know the places a horse might go. We'll be fine."

"I'd like to come," he insisted. "I know you're mad at me and would prefer it if I got in the car and disappeared, but I'd really like to stay and help you look."

It was my turn to feel embarrassed. He was right. I wanted him to go, but I also wanted him to come with us, find Firefly and save the day. He used to be my hero. I wished he could be a hero again.

Allison spoke up. "We can always use an extra pair of eyes, Mr. Rittenberg. Come with us and help us look."

Dad let out a breath I hadn't known he was holding.

"Let's go then."

After grabbing flashlights from the pile on Lois' desk we split up. Allison took the lead. We looked in the obvious places and all the narrow tracks around and through the woods.

We could hear chatter and laughter from campers beating the bushes for my horse, but for me there was nothing to laugh about. Firefly is old and much more fragile than people might think. With memories of Cricket's bout of colic driving me along, I looked feverishly in all the nooks and crannies we could find.

If Firefly had colic, he could be dying while we searched.

The longer we looked the more desperate I felt. My pulse was in my mouth, and the top of my head was going to blow off any second. Dad reached over and took my hand. He felt it shaking and stopped to look at me.

"I thought you didn't really like this horse," he said.

"Why are you so upset that he's missing?"

I couldn't answer, just shook my head and pulled Dad along. All the times I'd wished Firefly would die were whirling like a merry-go-round in my mind. What if I'd wished it one time too many and Firefly really was dead?

"I didn't mean it!" I yelled silently. "Please don't be dead!"

We were walking single file on a faint trail I'd never noticed before. I smelled horse poop and stopped dead. A great pile of the stuff sat wetly in the middle of the path. I stood aside and shone my flashlight on it so no one would make the mistake I'd almost made.

Dad and Allison went on ahead. I took up the rear, shining my light on the bushes lining the path. Nothing as big as a horse was hiding there, but I didn't want to take a chance and walk past him.

Something wet touched the back of my knee, and I cried out in fear. I know bears don't go looking for humans, but I'm small for my age and might make a tasty snack for a mama with cubs to feed. I didn't think my heart could beat any faster, but it did.

Whatever it was nudged my leg again, and I screamed and turned around to face my attacker.

"Yellow Dog!"

I bent down and hugged her as hard as I could. She

licked my face and smacked me with her furiously wagging tail.

"What are you doing here?" I asked stupidly. Like she was going to tell me.

I thought of all the times Yellow Dog had ambushed me in the woods. Usually she just wanted to play, but sometimes it was important. When Cricket was sick she looked for me and practically dragged me to where he was lying.

I listened then, and I was listening now. She sat in front of me and woofed.

Wherever Yellow Dog was, Cricket was never far behind. I didn't recognize this path but it had to be near his paddock.

By now the group had moved on and was far ahead. I gave the dog room to get in front of me and followed where she led.

The gate to Cricket's field was open.

First Firefly and now Cricket? Or was it the other way around?

I remembered what Ethel had said about Cricket: "He's an escape artist. He can open stall doors from the inside and, what's worse, he can open them from the outside, too. He loves to take other horses with him on his great escapes."

So where was he now?

Chapter Fifty-Nine

THE MOON WENT BEHIND A cloud, and all of a sudden it was pitch black. I needed something to keep me anchored to the path, so I hung on to Yellow Dog's collar. She whined and tried to lick my hand.

She led me to Cricket's tree, then pulled me around it to a patch of grass between the tree and the fence. Firefly was stretched out on the grass, and Cricket stood guard over him.

My chest got so tight I thought I was having a heart attack. I threw myself onto Firefly's neck.

"Don't be dead!" I sobbed. "Please don't be dead! I love you. I didn't mean those awful things I wished. Please wake up!"

It felt like the world was ending.

Cricket pushed me away with his nose and leaned down to nuzzle Firefly. Yellow Dog moved in closer and started to wash my face with her tongue. I'd never understood what the phrase "beside myself" meant, but now I could see myself, on the ground, crying my heart out.

Firefly shivered and tried to pick up his head. I rolled away and stood up. He got his legs underneath him and struggled to his feet, shaky, but definitely alive. I was shaky, too, but with relief.

I pulled Ethel's three carrots out of the waistband of my shorts. They were limp and bent out of shape, but Firefly noticed them immediately. He came over for a sniff and gobbled one out of my hand. Cricket stuck his head in front of Firefly's. I gave him the smallest, most crumpled-looking carrot and offered the last one to my summer horse.

I shouted to let Dad and Allison know where I was, then waited with an arm across Firefly's neck. I wasn't going to let him disappear again.

Dad came over and gave me a hug. It felt almost like old times.

We didn't have a halter or lead rope. I started to take off my shirt to use as a lead—I had an undershirt on! It wasn't like I was going naked—but Dad handed over his belt. I snugged it around the narrowest part of Firefly's neck and still had a bit to hold.

Cricket thought he was coming, too, but I pushed him back into his paddock and closed the gate. If he opened it there was nothing I could do to stop him, but he turned around and walked back to his usual spot under the tree. Yellow Dog, clearly conflicted about which way to go, stayed with her horse. Good choice, Yellow Dog.

We walked straight back to the barn, and Firefly seemed to get stronger with every step. I was weak with relief. My summer horse, my grumpy old reliable friend, was still alive.

Chapter Sixty

WE WERE THE FIRST TEAM back. Lois ran up with a halter for Firefly and returned Dad's belt to him.

She ran her hands all over Firefly's body and down each leg. She listened to his heart in three different places—including just above his left front hoof—then lifted his eyelids and peered into his eyes. She checked his mouth for an obstruction and even smelled his breath. Finally she poked her fingers hard into the side of his neck and timed how fast the dimples filled up.

Then she went to her office and called the vet.

I stood with Firefly in the aisle, gently stroking his neck. Did it feel good? Was it an annoyance? He didn't express an opinion, but his eyelids drooped and so did his lower lip. He seemed to be falling asleep.

Finally, Lois hung up and came over to me.

"Good job, Charley. You too, Allison."

She turned to my dad. "Thank you for helping with the search. You were a great support to the girls. They're not used to beating the camp bushes, let alone doing it in the dark. Your presence made it easier."

She smiled and reached out to shake his hand. Dad looked embarrassed, but he smiled back.

"In a cockeyed way it was fun," he said, as they shook hands. "I mean, I know it was serious—maybe even life or death—but being included in such an energetic and fearless search was a privilege."

He looked at us and smiled again. "Thank you for letting me lend a hand."

Dad put an arm around my shoulders and gave me a hug. I shrugged it off.

The other searchers straggled into the barn and bunched up in front of Lois. I could hear a quiet murmur, like a hive of bees might make after a hard day gathering nectar.

Lois cleared her throat.

"All right, ladies, Firefly is home safe and sound. We don't know how he escaped, but don't worry. We will. In the meantime, take this as an object lesson. If you ever work in a barn or have a barn of your own, know that evening barn check is the most important chore you do all day. An unlatched stall door can lead to disaster. Thank heavens, tonight had a happy ending. Now time for bed, all of you. Thank you for your help."

I WALKED DAD BACK TO his car.

I had to know. Was he really going to make me go home? I tried to clear the frog out of my throat.

"Uh, Dad." He stopped walking. "I don't want to leave with you tomorrow."

He started to answer, then stopped and started again.

"Charley. I don't want us to fight. I love you more than anything in the world, but carriage driving with Mrs. Calhoun sounds much too dangerous. When I think of what could have happened. . . ." His voice trailed off. "I just can't agree that it's safe. So, yes. I'd like you to come back with me. I'll help you pack in the morning."

I swallowed hard. Getting angry wasn't going to make him agree.

"I'll try to make you understand," I said. "Cricket is important to me. Learning to drive is important.

"Riding was so different from what I imagined that I just couldn't cope. I was so scared I made myself sick. Ethel stepped in when I was drowning. She took me home, cured my cough, and showed me what it's like to drive a horse instead of sitting on one. She cares about me and would never do anything to harm me."

I stopped. Dad wasn't really listening. He was still in the runaway carriage, terrified that I'd be hurt. What could I say to make him change his mind?

"Ethel isn't happy about what happened, either. She's started driving Cricket every day to make sure she doesn't have another freeze like that first one. In the beginning, her granddaughter sat in the cart to take the lines if she had to, but now Ethel's doing it as a sort of warm-up for my lessons. On the days I don't drive, she takes him across country just to enjoy the scenery."

Dad was listening now, and I relaxed a little.

"That first drive *was* scary, but I handled it. Being able to take charge, after weeks of being afraid and ashamed, has meant everything to me. It put me back together like nothing else ever has. It gave me back to myself."

Tears dripped down my face into my mouth.

"You have to let me stay. I need to be here."

He stared into my eyes for the longest time, then pulled a handkerchief out of his pocket and mopped up my tears.

"I hear you," he said finally. "You can stay."

Then he made a face like he did when I was a baby.

"You make sure you don't get hurt! You hear?"

I reached up to kiss him goodbye and was enveloped in his arms like the baby I still was, deep inside.

It felt wonderful.

Chapter Sixty-One

Dear Sally,

Sorry, sorry, sorry! Life at camp went from turtle-slow to jet-propelled, and I didn't have half a minute to write. I feel like the White Rabbit—always late! I'm not even sure what I've told you and what I haven't.

My first driving lesson . . . I know I wrote about that, but there have been many more since then. In the beginning I couldn't even hold the lines right, let alone the whip. Now I can harness Cricket up and even hitch him to the cart, so long as Ethel's around to keep an eye on the buckles and straps.

Camp isn't all about horses. Canoeing is my next favorite thing, and so far I've passed all the tests. I may even get an award at the end-of-summer campfire for "Keeping my Head." If you can believe it, I led a rescue mission when Horrible Jane fell out of her canoe without a life jacket.

Parents' Weekend is over, and I hope I never

have to go through another one. Dad came, but Mom went to Jeremy's camp instead. You can take it from there.

That's enough old news. Today I had an honest-to-God *adventure* driving Cricket. My hands are still shaking, so if my writing's wobbly you'll know why.

We were out for an afternoon spin to get the kinks out of all three of us. It wasn't a lesson, so Ethel did me a favor and held the whip. The hay had been cut, and we drove through barbered fields, just ambling along enjoying the ride.

For a change of pace, I turned down the middle of the field and kissed the air. Cricket flagged his tail and moved into a great big trot. When Morgans trot, even small ones like Cricket, they really cover some ground.

All of a sudden he gave a huge leap to the left, nearly tipping the cart over.

I turned a big half-circle to see what made him shy like that. Cricket isn't a spooky horse, so it must have been something serious. I imagined snake-armed monsters hiding in the tufts of grass.

No monsters, but a hole in the ground as big as an open grave.

It gave me the creeps just looking at it.

Ethel said it might be an abandoned woodchuck colony. Maybe when the haying machine went over the tunnels they collapsed. Whatever it was, I'm glad we aren't at the bottom of it.

Cricket was trembling. I handed Ethel the lines and got out of the cart. I rubbed behind his ears and looked into the hole.

Sitting behind him as we were, we wouldn't have seen it. And if it hadn't been smack in front of him, Cricket, wearing blinkers, wouldn't have seen it either.

Just the thought of what might have happened made my knees go all weak. I leaned on him until we both stopped shaking, then climbed into the cart and let Ethel drive us home.

So, what have you been up to?

Love,
Charley

Chapter Sixty-Two

NANCY AND I SAT ON the porch of Cabin One waiting for the call to supper. It had been a sad, sad day. I understood—really got it for the first time—that I wouldn't ride Firefly ever again.

I was keeping my hands busy, teasing the bark off twigs I'd found lying on the porch. I needed to do something—anything—to keep from crying.

"If I can't ride Firefly, I won't ride at all."

Sulky was better by far than Weeping Willow. A sliver of bark slid under my thumbnail and took my mind off my troubles completely. I stuck my thumb in my mouth, then took it out fast. How pathetic would that be, sucking my thumb and feeling sorry for myself!

"How many weeks are left?" Nancy asked. She proceeded to answer her own question by counting on her fingers. "Nearly three, I think. Maybe two and a half."

I said nothing, thinking of my bargain with Ethel. If I didn't ride, I couldn't drive. Without the time spent driving, I'd probably go mad. Then they'd send me home, and I'd never see Cricket again.

"I have an idea," said Nancy. "I'll just run it past Lois and see what she thinks."

She stood up, stretched, and trotted down the path to the barn.

I was too anxious to eat, but supper wasn't optional. They count heads. Nancy slid into her chair just before grace.

"Wait for me after," she said. "I have news."

All of a sudden the meatloaf smelled good.

WHEN SUPPER WAS OVER, I waited for Nancy on the porch.

"Let's walk," she said, swallowing the last bit of her Toll House cookie.

We followed the path past the camp horses' barn and ducked into the barn marked Boarders Only. It was definitely Off Limits, but obviously Nancy had permission to be there. We walked down the aisle and stopped in front of a dark bay giant hoping for handouts. He looked very pleased to see us.

"Hey, you!" Nancy said, digging a sad-looking apple from her pocket. "This," she added proudly, "is Thunderbolt."

I knew him as more than that. He'd been my friend in need. I stood on tiptoes to scratch his forehead.

Nancy stepped back and looked at him. "He is a little oversized," she admitted, "but he needs to be big to do his job." She gave his ears a rub and turned to me.

"You know I want to do three-day eventing, right?"

I nodded, but really, I didn't know the first thing about it.

"Well, Classic, much as I love him, is too small and, sadly, too old to do everything I need him to do.

"I just had a big talk with Lois, and she's going to lend me Thunderbolt for the rest of the summer. He's a Thoroughbred-draught horse cross, with the strength and size that's perfect for eventing. He's great across country, will jump anything, and he even likes dressage. Well, mostly."

I struggled for some way to respond to Nancy's excitement. "He's very handsome," was the best I could manage. And he was. But what did this have to do with me? I gritted my teeth against more tears.

Nancy smiled. "Classic has worked himself out of a job," she said. "And so has Firefly. I can see you're sad he's had to retire, and I know you're feeling a little panicky about the rest of the summer. If you can't ride

Firefly, what will you do?"

I couldn't speak.

"You can ride Classic!"

"Do you remember the day we met? I told you a little about Classic's history, about all the things he's done. He's been a racehorse, a polo pony, and a school horse. During the school year, he's a therapeutic horse in Fairlee's Riding for the Disabled program. He's been a star at all those jobs.

"You probably don't know how rare a horse like Classic is but, believe me, he's one in a million."

"But it's taken all this time to feel safe on Firefly!" I wailed. "How can I switch to a horse I don't even know?" I was spinning out of control.

Nancy patted my arm. "Firefly is a schoolmaster. His job is to teach by doing exactly what his rider tells him to do. He is what the student is. It can be frustrating, but it's a very good way to learn. When he finally gets it right, it's because *you* have.

"Classic is a different kind of horse. He loves to get with the program. He'll help you succeed in lessons and trail rides. He'll light up when you arrive and do everything he can to keep you safe and happy. He's never cranky. He's a good-time horse!

"Ride him in tomorrow's lesson and, if that goes

well, you and I will go on a little trail ride in the afternoon. Your confidence will soar, I promise."

NANCY WAS RIGHT. CLASSIC AND I danced through the lesson.

I couldn't keep the grin off my face, but I felt guilty. Was it wrong to enjoy riding Classic instead of grieving for Firefly?

I was so busy yakking to Nancy, I hardly noticed the trail ride. I even forgot how much I hate to post.

Of course Jane wasn't there, and nobody fell off, but I had a great time enjoying the scenery and listening to Nancy's horse stories. When she described galloping across country, jumping log piles and obstacles that looked like ships or houses, it was hard to believe we lived in the same universe.

Nancy's right. With Classic, everything we do is a blast. From now on, lessons are going to be easy. Make that double easy. Easy peasy!

I still miss Firefly. How could I not? He taught me everything I know. But he's a very serious horse, not a party animal like Classic and, with him, riding was not fun. With Classic, it's a party every day.

Chapter Sixty-Three

IT WAS TIME I LEARNED how to steer. Ethel said I never knew where my inside wheel was, and that, apparently, is a steering problem.

Here's what she did to fix it. . . .

Twelve traffic cones—witches hats, some people call them—were piled in the middle of the boarders' outdoor ring. Ethel set up six pairs of two, making an aisle of gates. My job was to drive down the aisle, make a big half-circle at the end, then go through them the other way.

Sounds dead-easy, doesn't it?

Cricket was fascinated by the cones. He wanted to sniff them, nudge them, paw at them, and knock them down. He had no interest in driving through them.

When I finally had him listening to me instead of his curiosity, I lined up the cart in front of the aisle of gates and asked him to walk—expecting a nice straight trip between the cones.

It took three tries just to get him to stay (sort of)

straight. The first time he knocked over all six cones on the right side. The second time he knocked over all six cones on the left side. The third time I started getting mad.

"What am I doing wrong?" I yelled at Ethel. "Why is he behaving this way?"

Ethel smiled.

"Shove over," she said, climbing into the cart. "You're discovering the power of a solid outside line. Putting it another way, you are learning what happens when your outside line is flabby."

Did I have any idea what she was talking about? Not one little bit.

I spent the rest of the summer finding out.

TODAY WAS GRADUATION DAY. TEN gates were arranged all over the boarders' arena. Each one had a big red number on the right-hand side. Clearance for the cart was one foot. Twelve little inches of space between my wheels and the traffic cones. Six inches on each side.

Cricket shone for all he was worth. His mane, combed and Brylcreemed within an inch of its life, floated in the breeze. His tail was a flag.

Ethel kept him moving while I walked through the gates for the last time. Then she stepped down and I stepped up.

I was on my own.

The plan was to drive through the gates at a collected trot, good and slow so I'd have plenty of time to look for the next turn. Cricket had other plans.

We flew.

By now I knew the route through the cones better than I knew my own name, but I had never driven it like this. A moment of panic that we were going too fast to steer dissolved into pure joy. Before we were through the gate in front of us, I was looking for the next one, and all Cricket needed was that look.

My eyes controlled my body, my body controlled the lines, and the lines controlled the horse. It was all one piece.

In one long, long second I was through the last gate, and it was over.

I looked up and saw Jane watching from the trees.

Chapter Sixty-Four

IT WAS THE NEXT-TO-LAST DAY at camp. I was on my way to Cricket's paddock, when Jane ran up behind me. I spun around, arms crossed, wearing the nastiest face I could muster.

"What can I do for you?" I snapped. I really didn't want Jane in my Cricket time.

Jane was excited, dancing from one foot to the other. "I want to show you something."

"Show me what, exactly?" I wasn't going anywhere, except to Cricket's field.

"It's a secret," she said. "Just come with me."

"You want *me* to go somewhere with *you*? Do I look crazy, or just plain stupid?"

I turned to go, but she ran around me and stopped with her face about half an inch from my nose. Ugh! I backed up in a hurry.

"Just a little trip. It won't take long. Anyway, you'll love it."

Jane started pulling at her hair. She was really

het up.

"You love it for me. I'm not going on any trips. Tonight's the last campfire. Carol will kill us if we're late."

"Please? Double please? Trust me. You'll like it."

"Maybe I would and maybe I wouldn't. But trust you? The only thing I'd trust you to do is make me miserable."

I've never seen Jane act like this. She seemed almost . . . normal. Except for the hair. Maybe it's a ploy. She'll lure me into the woods, tie me up, and leave me for the bears.

"Last chance," Jane intoned. "Going once, going twice, you're going to be sorry—"

"Oh, all right!" The words were forced out of me. "But it better be good."

She was off and running.

I caught up with her at the canoe dock. We signed out a canoe, and she grabbed paddles and two life jackets, making a face as she buckled hers up.

She took the stern seat. Jane never paddles in the bow.

"SO, TELL ME. I'M IN the canoe! Where are we going?"

"You'll see."

Yeah, I thought. *I just bet I will.*

We cut straight across the lake then turned to follow the shoreline. Eventually we came to a green-painted dock with two racks of canoes waiting on the sand. I read the name stenciled on the canoes: Green Mountain Sports Camp. My stomach clenched in a painful knot. This was not a place I wanted to be.

Jane beached our canoe, and we pulled it out of the water. She raised her chin and pointed to the left. I looked. Nothing there but trees and bramble bushes. She picked up the front of the canoe and started to drag it toward the trees.

"We'd better stash the canoe and move away from the dock."

I grabbed the other end. No point in leaving a trail that said "Kilroy Was Here!"

"You know this is out of bounds, right?"

Jane shrugged. "So?"

"So what are we doing here?"

"Just wait."

We snuck through the camp, ducking behind trees and bushes. A few boys walked around, but they didn't seem to notice us.

Do girls sneak into this camp often enough to

be ho-hum?

Jane walked up to the strangest building I'd ever seen: an enormous barrel had been cut in half lengthwise and was lying on its side. It was covered in corrugated metal and painted dark green.

She opened a door and my eyes went funny. The whole room was crooked, slanted—something. I blinked, and it came into focus. The floor was a wide oval track with an inward slope all the way around. In the middle, protected by a low fence, were bikes. A lot of bikes.

Jane smiled at me. Smirked might be a better word.

"Not what you expected, is it?"

I shook my head. "How did you find this place?"

"Last summer, when I was losing my mind with horse overload, I heard a couple of counselors talking. When I heard the word 'bikes,' I paid attention. I was desperate to ride something that wasn't out to kill me.

"I snuck out a canoe and paddled over here to have a look. I met some boys. They showed me where the bikes are." She looked smug. "The rest is history."

I shook my head. Jane making friends? With boys?

"Grab a bike." She pointed. "The shortest ones are over there, but any bike will do."

I was trying to decide between a red and a blue

Schwinn when the door opened and two boys walked in. I turned my back so they wouldn't see my face.

"Jane! Hey! Watcha doing?"

I froze. I knew that voice.

"Hi, Jem," said Jane. "I'm just here to show Charley how bikes can steer themselves."

I turned around, my face burning. "Hi, Jeremy." What else could I say?

"Charley?" Jeremy looked stunned. "What are you doing here?"

"I guess I'm here for a lesson in physics. How do you know Jane?"

"Physics?" He wrinkled his forehead. "I ran into her at the beginning of the summer." A dramatic pause. "She was trying to steal my bike." He grinned at her.

Well, that sounded like my Jane, all right.

"Why'd you steal his bike?"

"I only tried to steal it. He caught me before I could."

"But why?"

"So I could have something solid to ride, instead of stupid horses all the time."

"My front tire had a slow leak, and we fixed it." Jeremy looked at Jane. "She fixed it. I just handed her things. She's an ace bicycle mechanic. When she shows up guys bring her their bikes to fix. She's very popular around here."

Popular? Jane? Now I've heard everything.

"Can we move it along, please?" Jane's voice was at its snottiest. "We have to start back soon."

We left the bicycle hoard, taking the red Schwinn, and went looking for a suitable hill. Jane hung back.

"What's Jem to you?"

"He's my brother."

It's the only time I ever saw Jane at a loss for words.

The physics lesson was amazing. Jeremy took the bike to the top of a long, gently sloping hillside and gave it a shove. The bike rolled down the hill.

I expected it to fall over in the first ten feet but, every time it leaned, the handlebars turned and the front wheel moved back under the bike. Even though it was rolling on an uneven surface, it kept correcting its own steering.

It was eerie, like the bicycle was haunted.

Chapter Sixty-Five

"SO, HOW'S IT BEEN?" JEM didn't look at me while we walked. It was like he didn't want to read the truth on my face.

"It's okay. Not like I thought it would be, but okay. How do you like your camp? At least there are plenty of bike fanatics to keep you happy. Everybody probably smells of bicycle grease, just like you."

He changed the subject.

"I wonder how Sally's doing in Iceland."

I stopped dead. "How who is doing what, where?"

"Sally. You know, your best friend. Remember her? Red hair, long legs, looks like Pippi Longstocking without the braids?"

"What Sally's doing in . . . where did you say she was?" I felt totally disconnected from my tongue. From my brain, too.

Jeremy looked impatient. Slowly and carefully, as if he were speaking to an idiot, he started over.

"Iceland. An island nation in northern Europe near

Norway. Lots of volcanoes. They use thermal energy from all the underground hot springs. It's radical!"

I stared at him.

"What? I looked it up! What's wrong with that?"

I shook my head.

"She's going pony trekking with her cousins. No. Wait a sec. They aren't ponies. They're small horses. If you call them ponies everybody gets mad. The Vikings rode them, though their feet must have dragged on the ground."

"Sally's in *Iceland*? Why?"

"Snap out of it," Jeremy said. "You're sounding like a dodo bird. The cousin who was supposed to go broke her arm, and Sally was the only other cousin who could ride."

"Why didn't she tell me? I'm her best friend."

Jeremy rolled his eyes. "I have a bunch of letters from her back at my cabin. We can stop on the way and pick them up."

I was freezing cold and my hands had gone numb. "Where'd you get the letters? Mom brought them, right?"

His face turned red, but he nodded yes.

"For Parents' Weekend?"

Another nod. "Didn't Dad tell you?"

"That traitor? I didn't give him a chance to tell me anything. He's not coming home, so there's nothing to say." I felt a little guilty saying that. Dad hadn't been a total loss.

Jeremy stopped walking. "Dad's not a traitor."

"You're right. The traitor is Mom."

I walked away from him without a backward glance.

"Wait up!" he yelled. "Why be mad at me? I'm just the message boy! Anyway, you owe me. Whose idea was horse camp? All mine. You should be grateful."

Grateful! I put my head down and kept on walking.

Jeremy caught up and pulled me around to look at him.

"Grow up, Charley! Do you think you're the only person who's hurting? Like Mom and Dad dreamed up the whole divorce thing just to ruin your life? I'm hurting. Dad's hurting. Mom's hurting, too. A lot.

"So she didn't send Sally's letters. She wrote a forwarding address on the first couple and put them in a bowl near the front door to take to the post office. Then things got crazy and she forgot. She feels bad about it, okay?"

I stopped and gave him my dirtiest dirty look. "Just get the letters, okay? I'll meet you at the dock."

Chapter Sixty-Six

I LOOKED AT THE SKY, trying to gauge the time by the sun's position. We were going to be in trouble, big time.

"So," Jane said. "Physics."

"Jane, stop!" I held up my hand like a policeman. "Let's start paddling and you can tell me on the way back."

She took no notice.

"If you know how to ride a bike, you know about physics, even if you don't know you know. Say, for example, you're coasting down a long steep hill. The bike gets going too fast, so you slam on the brakes. What happens next—you flying over the handlebars— is physics."

"I don't care about physics! Let's get going."

"Everything in the world that moves is controlled by physics."

"So what? I want to get back to camp!"

I might as well not have been there. Jane just kept

on talking.

"With bikes," she said slowly, "what you put in is what you get out. Whatever you do is reflected in the bike. If you get it wrong, you might have an accident, but it will be your mistake. You can understand it.

"A bike doesn't start bucking like crazy, out of the blue, with no way to predict or prevent it."

"But you know what happened!" I said. "Jack plowed through a wasps' nest and got stung. That's why he bucked you off."

"If I'd been riding my bike, I might have been stung. I might have had a bad fall. I wouldn't have been bucked off."

She rubbed her left arm and made a face. "Horses are unpredictable. They spook, they run, they kick. I'll take a bike any day."

"But a bike can't love you," I said in a whisper.

"No horse has ever loved me," said Jane.

The words hit me like a fist in the solar plexus. I had Cricket. Jane had no one.

"I know what you mean," I said slowly. "Before camp, I *knew* any horse I met would love me. Then I met Firefly.

"There was no 'click.' That's what I expected. That we'd click. He didn't hate me or anything, but he wasn't going one step out of the way to help me. I couldn't trust him, and that made the whole riding thing scary."

No, that wasn't right.

"Not scary," I said. "Terrifying."

Jane looked away, clenching and unclenching her jaw.

"I'm not scared of horses. I just don't like them."

Her words were typical Jane, but I could see a tear sliding down her cheek. I scrambled for the right thing to say.

"But you're really brave. Every single day you get on a horse you don't trust and ride."

Jane fiddled with a strap on her life jacket, but she looked a tiny bit happier.

"I've always been scared of cantering. I'm afraid the horse will fall down with me." She stared into space. "When I was about six, my sister tried out a pony at a local show. They were cantering in a circle and the horse slipped and went down. My sister was thrown clear and wasn't hurt, but I can't get the picture out of my mind. If they buy me a pony, I'll have to learn to canter, and I know the horse will fall. I don't want to. I want to stay in the beginners' group where it's safe.

"The whole thing makes me really angry, and when

I get angry I start acting like my mother. I hate it, but I don't seem to be able to stop."

She gave me a quick look then focused on the view along the shore.

"I'm sorry I've been such a jerk."

Jane apologizing! I didn't know what to say.

"You're really good with bikes," I said, "and the boys here look up to you. Even Jeremy! If you never learn to canter, they can't make you show. You can study to be a bike engineer."

I could see Jane was chewing this over. "My mom will think of a way to make me learn to canter."

I scrabbled around for an answer. Jane was probably right. Then I had a vision.

"Your mother is like the Wizard of Oz, all smoke, sound effects, and empty threats. She doesn't have the power to make you learn anything."

Jane shook her head. "You don't know my mother."

"I know *you*, and I'd put my money on you any day."

I could see the cloud lift from Jane's forehead!

For a while we stood there without speaking, letting the words sink in.

"What about you?" Jane asked. "You're afraid of riding. Will you give up on horses altogether?"

"I'm not crazy about riding, that's true, but I still love horses. Maybe even more, now that I've actually met some."

I had to smile.

"Riding isn't my favorite thing, but I'm totally sold on driving. I love it. I love sitting behind the horse instead of on him. I love the feelings that come through the lines, straight from the horse to my heart. And most of all, I love Cricket. When I drive him, I feel brave and strong and like together we can do anything. Driving with Ethel is the best thing I've ever done."

Jane's smile was blinding. She held up her hand to smack palms, but instead of slapping, she clasped my fingers and held on to them.

"Then even with me being so mean this summer hasn't been a total loss?" Jane spoke with so much feeling I had to back up. "I'm glad. And I'm glad you found Cricket. You both deserve to be happy."

I was beyond amazed. Was this really Jane?

"Thanks for coming to see the bikes. You're the only one here who would understand."

"You're welcome," I said.

And the crazy thing? I actually meant it.

WE PADDLED BACK TO SECRET Lake facing into the wind. We'd left in what should have been plenty of time but were late anyway. Gloria was waiting at the dock, looking like an unexploded bomb.

She said nothing, just picked up our canoe, slung it onto the rack, and practically ripped the life jackets off our bodies. We ran for the cabin as fast as we could. I did, at least. Jane, back to being herself, just sauntered.

Chapter Sixty-Seven

ALL THE GIRLS HAD GONE ahead, and Carol was on the warpath. She waved her arm towards our trunks and said, "Get dressed. White shirt, green shorts. Hurry up. I'm going to the office to let Annette know you two are okay. When I get back you'd better be ready."

We made it to the campfire just in time. Evie had saved me a spot, and Jane slid in next to Debbie. Mrs. Behrens stood up to speak, and everyone scooted around to face her.

"This is a very special night," she started. "It's a night to reflect on the past, consider the present, and dream about the future. It's the night we each write our Letter to Self.

"First time campers often panic when they see the sheets of blank paper, but there's no need. You all know your stories already. Write what's in your hearts, and your letters will be perfect.

"Next year, if you come back to Secret Lake, you'll read this year's letter and realize how far you've come.

Then you'll write another Letter to Self to sum up another wonderful summer."

She stopped talking and sniffed the air. I sniffed, too, just to check. The most delicious aroma of roasting meat wafted into the campfire clearing. My mouth filled up with spit.

"Every year we talk about having a farewell banquet like the Welcome Dinner in June, and every year we decide instead to throw a full-on, over-the-top, Secret Lake barbecue: hamburgers, grilled chicken, corn on the cob, potato salad—the whole catastrophe. And I don't need to tell you what we're having for dessert. Anybody want to guess?"

"S'moooores!" we roared in answer. What else could it be?

The maintenance crew wheeled in two huge grills, already locked and loaded. They wore enormous padded gloves and crisp green-and-white striped aprons. We approached the food tables cabin by cabin. Thank goodness we were in Cabin One.

IN ABOUT NO TIME THE cookout was over. We sat in our groups so full of food it was hard to move.

Counselors from each cabin passed out thick white

stationary with "Secret Lake Camp" in green across the top. Matching envelopes had the name on the back flap. We were given clipboards and two sharpened pencils each. A battery-powered lantern was placed in the middle of each little circle for when it got dark.

All of a sudden I was sweating. Could I write about the hardest summer of my life? Could I be honest and tell a true story? How many hours would that take? Maybe the rest of my life.

I looked around the clearing. It was eerily silent. Everyone was head down over clipboard, writing steadily. Didn't they have to think?

The King of Hearts in *Alice* spoke quietly in my head. "Begin at the beginning and go on till you come to the end: then stop."

It seemed like a good idea.

Dear Self,

(Maybe it should be "Dear Charley." I peeked at Evie's letter, but her shoulder was in the way.)

I don't know what to say here, but since I have to say something I might as well make a start.

I didn't want to come to camp—not just Secret Lake, but any old camp. I wanted to stay home and keep the family together. No luck there. Mom wanted us out of the house and Dad, as usual, went along.

Talking didn't help, and neither did bawling like a baby. I tried a hunger strike to let them know I was serious, but it didn't work. We compromised with riding camp, so here I am.

If I had just one word to sum up the entire summer, it would have to be "surprising."

Not all surprises are good.

Being the only camper in the history of Secret Lake who didn't know how to ride didn't surprise me. I already knew. But everyone at camp, from the counselors and campers down to the cooks and the camp dog, saw it as a Really Big Deal. It put me in the spotlight, and I hated it.

Anyway, I was surprised my not knowing how to ride was such a surprise.

Then there was the horse surprise. I expected to love riding and adore my summer horse. Instead, I couldn't seem to bond with Firefly and was scared to death of riding. How could that be? I LOVE horses and wanted to learn to ride more than anything.

Cabin living was another surprise. I was counting on five instant friends who loved horses as much as I did. Instead, I got a pair of uninterested and unfriendly Barbie dolls, and Jane, a true monster in the making. Nancy was great, and Evie, who was new like me, wanted to be friends, but two out of five's not good.

I went to camp expecting friendship and became an outcast instead. Even my summer horse rejected me.

Then I met Cricket and everything changed. He's the horse of my dreams, a beautiful black Morgan with a gentle heart and a wicked sense of humor. He's smart and beautiful and he loves me.

Has this summer from hell changed my life?

You bet.

I had to learn to ride, no matter how much I wanted to give up. And I learned.

I had to bond with Firefly, even though he didn't really want to bond with me. And I did.

I learned how to lead. When the windy

paddle got dangerous, Birdie and I kept Jane from drowning both herself and Allie, and I held us together and safe until help arrived. I just did what needed to be done, but all of a sudden people saw me as a hero instead of a weight to carry.

When camp, and riding, and living with Jane got to be too much, I went to Ethel for help. And I let her help me. I'd never had to ask for help before.

I learned to keep going. No matter what happened, good or bad, there was no way out but through. I couldn't whine about it, either. If I'd been a whiner, even the few friends I made would have run the other way.

I was lucky. Ethel said it best. Cricket and Firefly are both extraordinary horses. To have known one is a gift. To have known them both is like my birthday all year round. I feel grateful to whatever power arranged for me to have such a great gift. I'm grateful twice that I had time to love Firefly as he deserves. If he'd died that night, I'd never have been able to let him know how much I love him.

When Carol came around with a lighter and a candle, I was lost in the story. The fingers of my right hand were stiff and sore, but I had a lot more to say. I scribbled as fast as I could.

Jane was the biggest surprise of all. She can act like a villain in a comic book, but there's more to her than that. Underneath, she's a sad, smart, funny girl whose passion is bicycles. How do I know? This morning she kidnapped me for a day at the boys' camp down the lake. They're all bonkers about bikes, and Jane is their hero. It seems she can fix just about anything to do with a bike. Even Jeremy looks up to her!

I saw a different side of Jane today, and I guess she saw a different side of me. She *forced* me to like her and—you know what? I do.

Who'd have guessed that would happen? Not me.

I looked around. Carol was dripping candle wax on the flap of Nancy's envelope. Nancy waited a second for it to cool, then pressed her thumb into the wax. "That'll hold it," she said happily. "And it's a perfect thumb print."

Bummer! Time's up and I haven't written about learning to drive! Or about Sally not getting any of my letters. Or about Dad and Parents' Weekend.

I never even found out why they call the bathroom the noss!

I squared up my eight (!) sheets of stationery, folded them, and put them in the envelope. As I pressed my thumb into the soft wax I made a wish to come back next summer and read what I'd written.

Somehow, some way, I will make that wish come true.

Love, Me

Chapter Sixty-Eight

THIS WAS THE DAY I'D been waiting for. My first solo drive. I'd been up half the night going over everything, and I knew exactly what I had to do. Now I'd just have to stay awake long enough to do it.

Cricket stood in the crossties looking sleepy. He was clean and shiny, his mane was plaited, and he was ready to go.

Ethel hung the harness on its hook and handed me the saddle. I laid it across Cricket's back and loosely buckled the girth. I straightened the back strap and the breeching and picked up his tail to put the crupper underneath it. I couldn't get over how he didn't seem to mind the crupper at all.

Next came the breastplate. I slid it over his head and put it in place across his chest. I buckled on the traces and criss-crossed them over the saddle to keep everything from sliding to the floor.

When I picked up the bridle, Cricket woke up and raised his head. I thought he'd start to play his stupid don't-put-that-thing-in-my-mouth game, but he meekly opened up for the bit. He stood quietly while I straightened his blinkers and buckled the throatlatch and the noseband. Then I slipped a halter and lead rein over the bridle.

That was as far as I got.

It was time to hitch Cricket to the cart—the time when it could all go wrong—and I just couldn't do it. Images of disaster raced across my personal movie screen. I froze solid.

I'd been helping Ethel harness and hitch Cricket for weeks. I could talk my way through it, write it down, even draw it. I should have been able to do it in my sleep.

Not today.

Ethel looked at me for a long time without saying a word. Then she went to stand at Cricket's head and waited.

I got the message. I could hitch the horse or forget the whole thing.

I stomped over to the cart, lined it up, and threaded one of the shafts through its tug loop. Ethel reached around to pick up the other and did the same. I clipped the quick-release latches to the breeching and tightened both girths. Then I threaded the lines through their keepers and coiled them on the seat.

I picked up the lines' buckle ends and fastened them to the rings of the bit. Then I unbuckled the halter and took it off.

I looked over at Ethel but her face was a mask. No help there.

Deep breath time.

We looked the harness over together and checked all the pieces out loud. Everything was where it should be and correctly done up.

Suddenly, I was as calm as ice.

"Forget something?"

Ethel's voice brought me back to myself. I checked everything again, fast as lightning.

"Nope."

"Check again."

Oops! I grabbed my helmet from its hook, twisted up my hair and jammed it on my head. My fingers were so stiff I couldn't make the buckle work. Ethel waited in silence.

Finally the helmet was on and fastened. I stepped up into the cart and settled myself on the seat. Then I arranged the lines in my frozen fingers, with the excess next to me on the seat.

I picked up the whip and shortened the lines until I

could feel Cricket's mouth.

He took a tentative step forward. Ethel cleared her throat, and he put his foot back where it belonged.

I squared my shoulders, checked that enough weight was in my seat bones, and took a deep breath. As I let it out, I whispered, "Cricket, walk up."

Nothing. Just a deep Cricket sigh.

"Cricket! Walk up!"

He lowered his head and walked out of the barn.

THE MORNING SUN GILDED THE trees and the dewy grass. The smell of pine needles stung my nose. I felt so light and happy I could have floated right out of the cart.

The route I'd rehearsed with Ethel followed my flight from that horrible first lesson with Firefly. Cricket walked briskly along the path, past the cabins and into the woods. He didn't like to walk. He was born to trot, and any second he was going to do it.

I got the word in first.

"Trr-ott," I said, as firmly as I could.

He was surprised. I could feel it, though I didn't know how. Maybe from his mouth down the lines to my hands. Maybe from his heart to mine.

I had a sudden vision of that trot getting faster, turning into a canter, and then a runaway, with me helpless in the cart behind him.

No way. I straightened my back, let out the breath I hadn't known I was holding, and made more weight flow into my butt. I was rooted to that seat.

Cricket kept on walking. Maybe I was *too* rooted.

"Trot up!" He flicked an ear in my direction and eased into a trot.

I couldn't believe it. There I was, all alone in the cart, trotting down the path with Cricket. Well, he was doing the trotting, but you know what I mean.

I've never felt anything like it.

I breathed in again, breathed out, and said "Whup, whup." Cricket slowed his trot, which hadn't really been very fast to begin with. "And walk, please."

I love the language of driving. Much more than riding, where you have your leg and seat to guide the horse, driving needs its own set of words. I'm always amazed when they actually work.

We walked for a while to let my heart slow down. Cricket could probably feel every heartbeat through the lines. The more relaxed I got, the softer his walk became. It was like being a Siamese twin.

We turned through the gate into the field where I

first met him. For me, it would always be Cricket's Field. Yellow Dog was waiting for us under the tree. She ran to the cart and trotted behind in the carriage dog position, between the wheels.

"And trot!"

We followed the fence line around the short side of the paddock. When we passed the second corner I took another deep breath (it was hard to remember to breathe) and shouted "Trot on!"

I know you're not supposed to shout, but I was so excited I couldn't help it. Cricket didn't mind. He sank down a little on his haunches and increased the power of his trot.

It was just like flying!

I slowed him down before the next corner. When I looked up for a sight of the gate, I saw my whole cabin, half of Cabin Two, and all the girls in Cabin Three hanging over the fence cheering. Carol and Lois were there, and even Gloria had showed up. Jane was against the fence, waving her arms and screaming. Jeremy stood behind her. He looked gobsmacked.

Off to the side, away from the mob, stood Ethel. Dad was next to her, beaming like the sun.

I grinned so hard my eyes were nearly shut and tears ran down my face.

I couldn't resist. Instead of slowing back to a walk for the gate, I kissed the air. Cricket kicked his trot up another notch and we zoomed down the long side at the speed of sound.

– THE END –

If you enjoyed *Charley's Horse,*
please write a review on the website
where you purchased the book.
Thank you!

About the Author

A native New Yorker, Judith Shaw married an Aussie and raised two children in Indonesia, Singapore, and the Blue Mountains west of Sydney, Australia. She has a deep love of animals and feels an almost psychic connection with dogs, horses, and, on one striking occasion, a pet python.

She was a solitary child. Her companion, caretaker, and best friend was Gamin, a black Standard Poodle known for hating the garbage man and cornering babysitters in the coat closet. Judith's first horse and the love of her life was a bay Morgan named Tom Thumb. When the family moved back to the States, Tom came too. At nineteen, he was probably the oldest gelding ever to cross the Pacific.

When a riding accident ended her love affair with horses, Judith focused on her other lifelong passion: writing. After decades as an editor and journalist, she began to explore fiction. *Charley's Horse* is her first novel. Judith lives in Berkshire County, Massachusetts with her husband Ron, and Tilly, her Jack Russell terrorist.

Read more of Judith's writing at
storiesbyjudith.com

Contact the author at
storiesbyjudith@gmail.com